Heaven Scent

John Winter

Nettle Books

This edition published 2015 by Nettle Books
nettlebooks@hotmail.com

© 2015 John Winter
ISBN: 978-0-9561513-6-0
Classification: Fiction

Second edition, 2015

CHAPTER 1

THE Sizzling Sixties, the Swinging Sixties, the Sexy Sixties. Charlie O'Flaherty was part of it, yet he wasn't. He had the key to the door but they had changed the locks. He could see vague shapes embracing through steamed-up windows, and hear wild music. He knocked on the door of the Sixties but no–one answered.

CHARLIE was compiling the horoscopes. It was a boring job and everyone on The Sandown Chronicle hated it. Except Charlie.

He also fancied the Editor's secretary, who was generally regarded as a dragon by other members of staff.

"What's your birth sign?" he asked.

"Taurus. Why?"

"I thought I'd write you a nice horoscope for next week," he said.

The editor's secretary was puzzled.

"How can you do that? It's pre-ordained, surely. Written in the stars. People study for years before they can interpret the signs and draw up a horoscope...."

"Pre-ordained by me," said Charlie.

He explained how it worked. The Chronicle had a master horoscope that they published every week for two years, and then they went back to the start.

"It's a bit dodgy because someone might notice, so I change bits around. I give people I like a happy forecast. Good isn't it!"

The Editor's secretary was shocked. "I call that fraud. False pretences. You can't do that!"

"I just did," said Charlie cheerfully. "Now I'm going to judge the weekly crossword competition. Fancy winning it?"

BUT let's start at the beginning, wandering along the beach of the quiet Isle of Wight resort. The sands, which had shifted impatiently under the relentless pressure of winter gales, were now wide and empty. Waiting. A fisherman plodded slowly out towards the surf in search of tomorrow's bait, his footprints slowly filling, swallowed by the rising tide.

In Sandown High Street, a gangling youth leant against the wind as he delivered the Green 'Un, his thoughts half a year away; he lay with a freckled girl, their flesh soaking up the heat of the dunes. But summer was long gone. Their romance had cooled as the first chill winds of autumn dusted sand over the promenade.

A ragged newspaper, stained with vinegar and heavy with squashed chips, cart-wheeled along the street and dived into the shelter of a butcher's shop door, temporarily distracting Tim Smith as he attempted to undo Thelma Hopkins' bra through a vest and a heavy woollen cardigan. His heart wasn't really in it – how could it be when she was sucking a throat sweet and constantly sneezing? Her nose had left a shiny trail on his shoulder.

Most shops were locked up, and would remain so until the arrival of the first coach-loads of old folk on cheap Spring breaks in a few weeks time, to be followed quickly by the summer crowds. The mischievous wind crept in through trembling doors and rattled window frames, chasing dust and paper scraps around the bare floors.

A rusty paddle steamer pitched wildly in the rough sea as it headed out of the bay after picking up a few dispirited visitors from the rusting and ramshackle pier-head landing stage. They huddled in the tiny bar that sat like a shed in front of the chimney stack, unable to see out of the smoke-grimed windows. In the summer the Sandown Queen did brisk business, but now it was hardly worthwhile running a service.

Two youths picked their way through a dark little changing room at the rear of the pier pavilion. The wind must have blown the door open, they saw their chance, and nipped in. After all, there might be something nickable, and no–one was likely to be in there in the winter when the pavilion was hardly used.

"Bit of a junk room," remarked one, surveying a jumble of crumpled cardboard boxes, old newspapers and empty tins. Then they spotted the green bottles, on a dusty shelf in the darkest corner, furthest from the door. They wouldn't have bothered but for the smell. It was, said one, like boiled rhubarb. The other was reminded of candy floss, a wood fire, and Angela Braithwaite's hair – in fact, all his favourite smells.

The cap on one bottle had popped off, and the contents overflowed down the side. "What does the label say?" asked the young romantic. "Heaven Scent" said the other.

They decided it must be after-shave or perfume. They couldn't carry all the bottles, so they left with an armful each, jamming the door closed behind them.

IN the absence of old Pottsie (Sir Humphrey Potts, chairman of Sandown Newspapers and a leading local magistrate, who was presiding in court) and Iron Balls (Mr Ian Ball, the editor, who was playing golf), Charlie represented the resort's weekly newspaper, The Chronicle, at the annual cheese and cocktail bash of the Sandown Regatta Steering Committee at the Royal Pier Hotel, on Pier Street.

The committee were not very happy about it. They felt strongly that the committee was important enough to deserve the presence of an executive, not a reporter.

The editor's secretary had feared Charlie would let the newspaper down. He hadn't shaved and had a hangover. "Don't say Mr Ball is golfing, tell them he's at a meeting of the Guild of Editors," she said.

"Fear not," replied Charlie, "I will be as discreet as a nun's fart."

The editor's secretary winced. She wished she worked for a posh publication, like Woman's Weekly or National Geographic, where male editorial staff wore cravats and drove MG Midgets and washed occasionally.

And so the Regatta Committee mingled and gossiped and sipped their G&Ts, while a string quartet and pianist played softly in the background. They all agreed the music was quite inspiring.

Charlie, in his work pullover, and the blue trousers with the kebab stain down the front, insisted on a pint of beer, not a bottle, not a lager, a pint of hand-pulled, and stood there, alone, in the middle of the room. He stood out like a bulge in a bishop's trousers, his presence widely noted, but no-one quite sure how to acknowledge it.

At last the committee's social secretary approached. She ran the second largest estate agency in town.

"Can I help you with any information?" she asked.

"No thanks, just listening in," replied Charlie, giving her the once over. He quite fancied the crisp, freshness of professional women.

She was about 10 years older than he was, tall and shapely, in a short, tailored light-green suit, and a blouse with a frilled collar – nicely furnished with full bay windows and ensuite facilities, if you like.

"We did hope to see your editor... is he busy on the front page or something?" she said vaguely.

"Nope, he's on the golf course," said Charlie, who felt he had no obligation to hide the facts. He was inspired to take her across the grand piano, his knees thumping out the cannon suite of the 1812 overture, her hair falling in disarray.

She tossed her head prettily and wandered off.

There was a brief discussion about the arrangements for the Regatta, but it was all very boring and middle class, so Charlie finished his beer and faded away, and everyone was grateful for that, except the social secretary who was inspired to think, quite guiltily, what it would be like to have sex with him, upright, thrusting across the booming strings of the double bass.

CHARLIE rubbed Smithy's ears. The dog liked him.

Smithy – part Chow, part Labrador, part Mongol warrior – belonged to Tim, who was a fellow journalist on the Chronicle.

Charlie liked Smithy, which was unusual, as he normally hated dogs. He took an immediate dislike to the editor's poncey poodle Meacha.

Smithy, on the other hand, would have had a wild time with Meacha. It was, after all, the Liberated Sixties. Meacha, however, wanted something Smithy couldn't provide, pedigree and class.

"That's a very pretentious name… Meacha," Charlie said to the editor's secretary, who was also after a bit of class, which didn't include Charlie.

She was looking after the dog while the editor had a business lunch. "I quite like it," said the secretary, who was named Primrose.

"To me, she looks more like a Pongo," said Charlie.

Primrose shuddered. So did Meacha.

IT was a Thursday, the day the Chronicle is published at 5pm, or thereabouts, give or take an hour or so, depending on last-minute advertisements, late front page stories and the inclination of Red Harry Hawkins, the machine room overseer, who might still be enjoying a liquid lunch in the 'Landlady's Arms' next door.

The Frog and Trumpet is a very hospitable hostelry, particularly to staff at the Chronicle, and even more so to Harry, who has a thing going on with Daphne, the landlord's wife.

As a matter of interest, the link between the two (pub and newspaper, not Harry and Daphne) is so close that the emergency button in the office lift is linked to the Snug bar. Press the button five times and five pints of Burt's Best Ale are lined up when the reporters arrive. Nice isn't it!

Tim Smith, the crime reporter, was busy – by Chronicle standards – because there had been a cliff rescue the night before, and by the time he had taken down the details from police and coastguard, and phoned his copy over to the evening papers, he was running late in writing the story for his own paper.

Tim was 23. Single. His main exercise was walking Smithy, who ruled the house and didn't like visitors. Including girlfriends.

"Why don't you get a nice mature girlfriend who likes dogs?" his aunt Mabel had suggested. She was his closest relative, his mum having died a few years before. His dad had run off with an Avon lady when Tim was very young.

"I can't find any. It's as simple as that."

"And those you go out with are too young, like little Thelma. She's scarcely left school, and very shy," scolded his aunt.

Not that shy, thought Tim.

7

"How did you get on with that Thelma?" Charlie was saying..

"She had a cold. And she wouldn't go in the house when she heard the dog howling. It's getting bad when the only dates I get are with girls who have cold sores," Tim grumbled.

"At least you get dates. I haven't had one for years," complained Charlie.

Picture this – a dark haired bloke, a shade over 6ft 3ins tall, with a good jaw, taut stomach and buttocks, medium build, slightly bigger right shoulder than left because of the badminton and tennis, blue eyes and a smile that turns the mouth up at the corners. Hugely attractive to women.

That's not Charlie. He wasn't an attractive prospect...

He had no dress sense, long, limp hair, and a spotty complexion. He liked girls but didn't know how to talk to them. He didn't find small talk easy and tended to panic in one to one situations. Charlie was thin as a whippet, had no interest in sport, and liked his beer too much, which caused problems.

DRUNKEN JOURNALIST, 26, KNOCKED PC's HAT OFF.... that sort of thing.

But he had a keen eye for the quick profit.

When Tim arrived for work that morning – late as usual, this time because Smithy had chewed the bell off the alarm clock – Charlie was in the Chronicle reception area talking to an earnest young man wearing a black armband.

Tim paused to listen.

"It's Mr Williamson, isn't it?" he asked.

"No, Wilkinson. Ernest Wilkinson."

"How can I help?"

"Well, my mother died..."

"...and you want to put in a funeral report?" interrupted Charlie.

"No, that was in last week's edition. It was very nice. Now it's my father Horace... he died this morning, of a broken heart I think."

"Great!" said Charlie, with undisguised enthusiasm.

HEARTBREAK HORACE DIED OF GRIEF – he could see the headline.

"I would hardly describe it as 'great'," said the young man, standing up, clearly offended.

"Sorry, Mr Williamson, I was not, of course, referring to your father's demise, merely the newsworthiness of the story."

"Wilkinson," said Mr Wilkinson.

"And I was indicating how nice it was that the couple could be back together so soon, mourned, but married in death so to speak."

"That's very nicely put," said Mr Wilkinson, sitting down again. "Would you write it down? I'd like to have that on the gravestone..."

"I'm afraid that's copyright," said Charlie.

Tim could hardly believe it. Here was another of Charlie's scams.

"Copyright?" said Mr Wilkinson, well and truly hooked.

"Yes, everything written or conceived in the Chronicle office is our copyright and cannot be reproduced without permission and payment of a small fee."

"How much?"

Tim thought it time to interrupt.

"Charlie...."

He looked round, irritated. It wasn't the money, it was the satisfaction he got from doing it. – "Just a moment, I am talking to Mr Williamson..."

"Wilkinson," said Tim and Mr Wilkinson, in unison.

"The copyright laws have been changed..." Tim said, determined to sabotage his swindle once and for all.

Charlie gave in graciously. Mr Wilkinson thanked him for the free inscription, and started to dictate details of his late father's life for the death report. Obituaries was the most popular page in the paper.

CHAPTER 2

IT's not surprising that Charlie had a flair for memorial verses, because about 20 years ago his uncle Ernest and Aunt Edna were killed in an accident, and Charlie made a point of putting a new memorial poem in the Chronicle each anniversary of their deaths. It was quite touching, really, but the O'Flahertys were a close family.

Ernest O'Flaherty had been a bit of an inventor.

In his youth, he invented the polystyrene cricket box. It was light, cheap and disposable.

They were mass produced by a local manufacturer, but are now just a painful memory, having an obvious shortcoming, their frailty. It was with tears in the eyes that Horace Oglethorpe, a neighbour who had volunteered to test the new box, was helped to the pavilion, retired hurt, with white polystyrene flakes billowing from the legs of his trousers – "First time I actually knocked the stuffing out of someone," remarked the bowler uncharitably. However, the factory did well, discovering a market for them as Chinese take-away plates (remember that, next time you eat off one.)

And then Ernest, after a brief philosophical debate with his bookmaker about the over-population of the Third World – "I bet there are more Chinese than Indians" – turned his attention to birth control.

His spray-on condom (it avoids all that fumbling about) might have worked wonders had he not sought to experiment with it on a woman of the streets.

While he was trying to get his boots off, she mistook it for hair lacquer and sprayed it all over her head. What a to-do! It was only his quick action in cutting breathing holes through the thin rubber film across her face that saved her life. Thereafter he used it to cover his bike.

Whatever next? Ernest had no shortage of ideas, usually manufacturing his devices on dubious licenses granted by shadowy foreign officials, but sadly experienced failure with an elephant muck spreader (it raised a stink in Delhi), a home circumcision kit, which bit off more than it could chew in Jerusalem, and the electric socks that so unfortunately cremated a Buddhist in Sri Lanka.

All in all, he hadn't been a great success, and he was lucky to have kept out of jail, but the Town Council thought differently. Possibly influenced by a wave of sentiment that followed his tragic death, and the fact that he had been a former Mayor, not to mention a generous donation from the Chinese take-away plate manufacturer, they put up a statue to his memory on the esplanade.

"He was a bit ahead of his time," Charlie explained to Tim. "Some of his ideas would have been quite good – a mobile phone, for example."

"What's that?"

"A phone you carry around with you, so you don't have to find a phone box. But it would have been difficult to make – too big and heavy, I reckon. Who would want to carry around a phone? And where would you plug it in?"

"It would never have taken off... a bit like that rocket," said Tim.

Charlie had explained the circumstances of Ernest's death to Tim. His uncle had become obsessed with a new interest, launching model rockets and developing rocket fuel. – "I was only a kid, but I remember him down on the pier, launching that last one. It was the highlight of the annual regatta – big crowds all along the front, and on the cliff paths, the fireworks, and then the spotlight on the landing stage at the end of the pier, where my uncle and aunt were igniting the rocket," he said.

"It was a fat, stumpy rocket, about six foot tall, and it worked. A glow spread out from underneath, wider and wider until the whole of the pier and the boats on the water were lit up, and then a ball of green light growing bigger and bigger and reaching higher and higher until we could see the rocket leaping up into the clouds. It was really good. Went up about a mile, they said, before it broke up. No–one ever knew why it didn't work."

He fell silent. They were sitting in the Frog and Trumpet, supping pints. Tim watched Daphne's breasts – she was bending as she washed glasses behind the bar. She knew he was watching. She meant them to be watched. Indeed, if ever breasts were meant to be washed, sorry, watched, these were they... or should it be them?

Charlie was oblivious to anything.

"They died together, arms around one another. They must have seen the bits of rocket coming straight back down, and held each other close for the last time. It's a story straight out of a front page. COUPLE LINKED ARMS AS WAITED FOR DEATH. All that was left were a few charred remains, and his bike, which was virtually untouched."

"That spray on condom must have been good stuff," ventured Tim.

They didn't talk much after that. Charlie was full of his memories, and Tim was licking beer foam out of Daphne's navel, mentally anyway.

The buzzer sounded from the Chronicle lift. Daphne put her coat on and left. No-one should have been in the office at that hour, so presumably it must have signalled an assignation with Harry.

"Do you want another?" Tim asked, not bothered that much, now Daphne was gone.

Charlie wasn't listening. He was still back with Uncle Ernest, blown apart on the pier.

"INVENTOR BLOWN UP OUT OF ALL PROPORTION," Tim mused. But he didn't say it.

CHAPTER 3

SANDOWN was unusual in the fact that it had a sea police patrol. It was the work of Horatio Blunder, the local chief of police who, as his name suggests, came from a long line of seafaring folk (he liked to suggest they were Royal Navy but in fact they were local fishermen).

He was quite small for a bobby, and tubby, and never stopped talking, and interfering, as if to make up for his lack of physical presence. He had thick, black curly hair that he liked to backcomb, so it made him look taller. Blunder managed to get the police authority to buy his force a little outboard motor boat. It was useful, but it put HM Coastguard's nose out of joint.

The sight of a couple of policemen in full helmet phut, phut, phutting around the end of the pier in their little boat was a source of ribald comment from local youths and from Dare Devil Leslie, the one-armed pier diver, who would target them with a bucket full of fish heads if he got the chance.

Blunder was in his 50s and ready for retirement, so he liked a nice, quiet, orderly ship.

"Anything doing?" Tim asked at the police station morning press call.

Pc Cartwright, a thin, sallow youth, flicked through the incident book.

"Couple of drunks."

"Not Charlie again?"

"Nope, he's being a good boy at the moment. A stolen car radio, and undergarments of assorted colours nicked from the washing line at the Frog and Trumpet."

"That Daphne is an alluring creature," Tim agreed.

Pc Cartwright took a mouthful of cornflakes from a bowl on the desk.

They were interrupted by a shout from Blunder in the back room – "What was that?" he bellowed.

"What was what?" said Cartwright, mouth still full, quickly placing the bowl in a drawer.

"That booming noise. Quite distinct. Came from the back of the station – might have been the coastguard's signal rocket...."

To Blunder's credit, no-one else had noticed it. He came out into the reception area, straightening his police tie (it had little white handcuffs in diagonal stripes on a blue background). "Get on to the coastguard and check it out. If it was the maroon, we need to be out there helping in the rescue," he said. "If there's trouble, they know they have to turn to the professionals."

On duty at the coastguard station, the coastguard was finding it difficult to concentrate. He had his telescope on a young woman of blossoming age who was walking her dog on the beach. He couldn't make out what the fool on the telephone was saying. Sounded like he was chewing a telephone book.

"I said..." gulped Pc Cartwright, though his cornflakes "I said, did you...." he swallowed and the soggy mass vanished "... fire the signal rocket?"

The coastguard only heard the last part.

"OK, message received," he said, reluctantly dropping the telescope, and putting down the phone. "George," he shouted to the junior coastguard, "fire the signal rocket. Someone must be in trouble on Culver Cliff. We need the cliff rescue team."

Pc Cartwright stared blankly at the receiver. He wasn't quite sure if the coastguard had understood him. He was about to ring him back, when there was an explosion in the sky that rattled windows all over the resort. - "There you are," said Blunder, "I told you it was the maroon."

Members of the cliff rescue team reacted as any well-trained force – they instantly stopped what they were doing (unless there was sex or money involved) and headed as quickly as possible for Culver.

Beryl Bloggett, the well-known local traffic warden and amateur fortune teller (she was usually pretty good at knowing what was round the next corner, but not on this occasion) was innocently pursuing her rounds on Sandown Esplanade when she was knocked off her moped by a charge of bread vans, coal lorries, an ice cream van and several private cars – all intent on being first to the cliff top.

Her enthusiasm for the future prospects of others remained considerably dented for some time, as did her bike.

"That's our traffic warden," observed Pc Cartwright as the back draught from the police van tumbled her back into the gutter from which she had just risen.

"Should know better than to cause an obstruction," observed his superintendent, sourly.

Oddly, they passed a fire engine heading in the opposite direction, siren wailing.

"Stupid fools. They never get it right," snarled Blunder.

If he had looked through the back window he would have seen a pall of smoke hanging over the town.

"Actually, there's a fire back..." started Pc Cartwright.

"Too busy for that now," snapped Blunder, and they raced blindly on.

The sky darkened and it began to rain.

On the cliff all was confusion. There was no obvious sign of anyone trapped and an argument was going on between Red Harry of the Chronicle's machine room, who was also Father of the Chapel for the printer's union, and his boss Sir Humphrey Potts, the previously mentioned newspaper boss and chairman of the Cliff Rescue Action Partnership, a fund raising group of local do-gooders, whose letterheads bore the unfortunate abbreviation C.R.A.P.

"I tell you it's my turn to go down," snarled Sir Humphrey. At 65, only three things stimulated his adrenalin – the excitement of cliff rescues, the power he wielded in industrial confrontation with his workers, and the sight of his wife Dorothy's bosom. She was 30 years his junior.

Staff at the Chronicle hated him.

Only the previous week he had, whilst walking through the editorial room, slapped Millie (the court reporter) upon the bottom as she bent to extract a globule of Charlie's chewing gum from her shoe, exclaiming rudely: "You won't find any news down there, my girl!"

Millie stood up, flushed with anger and embarrassment - "Keep your hands to yourself," she said.

"Just remember who you are, " he'd retorted, scowling at the rest of the editorial team as he departed.

"POTTS HAS HOTS FOR BOTTS," commented Charlie.

Sir Humphrey had been in the cliff rescue team since his youth and usually had the glamour job, dangling on the end of a rope to carry out the actual rescue. The Chronicle had devoted hundreds of column inches to his exploits.

"CHRONICLE BOSS IS RESCUE HERO" screamed the headlines several times every summer. In the winter, with less visitors around, there were a lot fewer rescues to make. Nonetheless, Sir Humphrey's photograph regularly appeared in the paper, often at one of his public engagements, opening fetes, presenting cheques. Only last week there was a picture of him at a local nursery school, bouncing a runny-nosed infant on his knee as he handed over toys from the Rotarians. "POTTS COPS TOT'S SNOT" was the headline Charlie suggested, but the subs dissuaded him.

In fact, until Red Harry came along, no-one else wanted to go down the rope. It was, after all, dangerous. There was always the option of calling in a rescue helicopter, but Sir Humphrey was reluctant to do that because he liked the glamour of the job, the public acclaim.

There was now, however, a growing realisation that Sir Humphrey was getting too old for the job.

"He's getting too old for it, " Lady Dorothy confided to her sister-in-law, who completely misunderstood her, and went home spreading rumours about his lack of virility.

"He's getting too old for it, " said Harry when his boss agreed a pay deal for the Chronicle staff that gave them increases above inflation, when usually he had to fight tooth and nail to get any rise at all.

"He's getting too old for it," wheezed a young man who, after becoming trapped on the cliff face, had to rescue his rescuer, Sir Humphrey having knocked himself out when the zip on his fly snagged on the abseil rope, swinging him wildly out of control into an overhanging rock.

Harry, on the other hand, wanted to impress his men with his bravery. He didn't see why a member of the privileged classes should get all the glory.

A thin, whiplash of a man, he was a union official of the old school. "By the rule book, by the rule book" was his catch phrase in Chapel meetings, and although the printer's union nationally had lost much of its power Harry still acted and negotiated as if nothing had changed. "Are you a Communist, Harry?" enquired Charlie once, over a pint in the Frog and Trumpet.

"What's one of those, Brother? We're all Socialists today," replied Harry, all innocence. They suspected his sympathies remained very much to the Left.

His men were grateful for the successes he gained, but these had to be weighed against the niggling strikes and go-slows he still attempted to introduce. They were not happy to lose wages pursuing his ideological fantasies. They applauded him publicly, but sniggered at his extremism behind his back.

Anyway, back to the cliff top. The printers watched sullenly as Sir Humphrey was harnessed to a stout rope and lowered over the edge by his supporters.

"Shall we go back to town?" said one, hopefully. It was becoming quite cold. There was sleet in the rain and the wind was strengthening.

"No we won't - that old windbag is looking in the wrong place," said Harry. "Most people get stuck on the chalk slope – we'll 'ave a look over there."

So the printers fetched another rope and Harry went over the edge about 250 yards away from where his boss was bouncing around, swearing at the seagulls. Their eyes met. Sir Humphrey shook his fist.

Flint and boulders fell away under Harry's scrambling toes. He pushed himself across the slope, searching. No–one was there. Two gulls flew at him, screeching angrily.

It was 2.15pm. Harry realised his men had missed their lunch break. If he continued his search and then they pulled him up, it would be nearly 3pm and they would have missed out on a tea break as well.

"Take a break," he bellowed, his words torn away by the gale. "I'll keep looking."

One of his companions waved an acknowledgement. They rammed a stake into the soil and secured his rope to it, retiring to a newspaper van for refreshment.

Harry moved crab-like across the cliff face. He was beginning to think it was a false alarm. The gulls were getting more aggressive. He grabbed a tuft of grass and defended himself with his little red rule book.

Back in the warmth of the police van, Pc Cartwright was losing interest. "This is a dead loss – there's obviously no-one trapped, and something's happening back in town. You can still see the smoke," he said.

"We have to be sure. We are here to protect the public," said Blunder, pompously.

"If you called out a helicopter, they could search the whole cliff in a few minutes."

"We only do that in a recognised emergency. It costs us money – we are, after all, protectors of the public purse."

But after a few more minutes Blunder had had enough.

They went to the cliff edge. "It's no good, nobody's here," Blunder bellowed down to the newspaper boss, who had ceased any pretence at a search and was slowly rotating in a clockwise direction.

By the time they hauled him up Sir Humphrey's normally pink face had turned a greeny-grey with cold and fatigue. "I'm getting too old for this, " he said. "Who's the fool who sounded the alarm?"

Pc Cartwright shifted uncomfortably.

They helped Potts to an ambulance, as his legs wouldn't work.

As they passed the newspaper van, a printer popped his head out and asked:" Is that it? Can we pull Harry up?"

There was a sadistic streak in Sir Humphrey. "Oh, you're a bit late," he said. "They've already fetched him up. He's on his way to the hospital to thaw out."

"Poor old Harry," they said.

"Poor old Harry" indeed! He shouted and screamed at the sound of the rescue convoy leaving the cliffs. But his cries for help were torn from his lips by the wind and dashed to pieces between the crushing indifference of the breakers below, and the blind, immovable apathy of the mud and rocks around him.

Sir Humphrey chuckled to himself all the way to hospital.

TIM found Charlie surveying the wreckage of a car and garage in The Broadway. Firemen were damping down the smoking ruins. The only policeman in sight was Sgt Derek Watson, who had the misfortune to be the owner of the property devastated by what had obviously been a major explosion.

He stood there looking up at the chimney of his house, from which was suspended a bent TV aerial crowned by a steering wheel. A lawnmower handle protruded from a hole in the roof.

"It must have been a bomb. it could only have been a bomb," he muttered.

"What about a gas leak," suggested Charlie helpfully.

"Or your petrol tank... you weren't messing about welding it or something like that, were you?" said Tim.

"I wasn't anywhere near the car, luckily for me. I put it in the garage about half an hour before. And we don't have any gas in this road. It can only have been a bomb."

Blunder appeared, and noisily started to organise everyone. "You two reporter chappies, clear off. Especially you, O'Flatly. You are hampering a major investigation," he said.

"It's O'Flaherty. Not Fart, not Flat, O'Flaherty," said Charlie, irritably.

"I don't care how you say it, clear off."

They ignored him. He pretended not to notice and bustled off to order the fire brigade around. The firemen ignored him too.

Charlie wondered why it had taken the police so long to turn out.

Tim told him about the false alarm on the cliff. "The bang that Blunder heard must have been the car exploding, and not the signal rocket. It all got very confused."

"It usually does when he's around."

"What's that odd smell?"

Faintly, above the pong of burning rubber, there was, indeed, a strange, eggy aroma.

Mr Watson Snr, the Sgt's aged father, sucked on his pipe for a moment, and looked suspiciously at his grandson, who had been listening intently.

"Bit like peaches," said Charlie.

"It's probably the smell of that after-shave I gave you," said young Bogey Watson.

Sgt Watson had heard the bottle of Heaven Scent bumping around on the back shelf of the car just before he got home.

"I didn't even have a chance to use it, not that I wanted to; it smelt horrible," he said.

"Cost me loads," lied the lad, sulkily. "Anyway, why should anyone blow up our car?"

"Better call out the bomb squad," offered Charlie.

That's a good angle for the story, Tim thought. And it was.

TERRORIST LINK TO BOMB BLAST screamed the Chronicle headline that evening. There was a picture of the debris, and another one of Sir Humphrey, in his official capacity as chairman of the police committee, beaming broadly, as if the carnage was something to be proud of.

They even beat the local evening papers to the streets, which may have had something to do with the fact that the printers co-operated fully in the absence of their leader Harry 'Awkins, who had finally been retrieved and hospitalised suffering from exposure and bird bites.

He was lucky to have been found at all. It was just before dusk fell that the head coastguard, back at his observation post after the anti-climax of the false alarm, scanned the beaches searching for the nubile dog walker he had seen earlier. Noticing unusual excitement amongst a flock of gulls on the cliff, he sent a young coastguard out to investigate... and there was Harry, still swinging.

"Wish I'd left him there, all he did was moan. Wanted me to search for a rule book, or something. All I could find was torn bits of paper," said his rescuer.

CHAPTER 4

CHARLIE and Tim had figured prominently in the local newspaper headlines the previous spring. The Chronicle, of course, didn't use the story. "We are not into the habit of making ourselves look ridiculous," sneered the editor.

It all happened because of the Great Sandown Flying Machine Race, an annual event that was regarded by many as the highlight of the Spring Regatta. The idea, quite simply, was to design a machine that would out-distance all competitors in a flight from the pier head.

No-one remembered who thought it up, although it might have had something to do with a local playboy who once took his girlfriend up for a flight in an old bi-plane, and showed off by flying right under the pier before copulating on the beach. It was a feat that was never to be repeated. The flight, not the copulation.

Anyway, there was a lot of rivalry between regulars at the Frog and Trumpet and the Irish lot at Murphy's Tavern in the town centre. Not content with fierce competition over pool, darts and dominoes – and the claim by barmaid Mad Maggie Flynn that she could arm-wrestle to the floor anyone the Frog and Trumpet cared to nominate – it was decided to compete against one another in the flying machine contest. There was, actually, more than honour at stake, for the top prize was £30 and the winning two-man team, traditionally, were entitled to drink free in any alehouse in the town for a week.

Charlie and Tim were nominated to represent the Frog and Trumpet. "What about Harry?" Tim said, not that keen.

"Sorry, mate, but I have to be always on call for the cliff rescue team. They can't do it without me," he said. Modest bloke, our Harry. Daphne smiled proudly upon him.

Now, Tim might not have been everyone's idea of a heartthrob, but – in the years before Smithy took over the house – he had been a man of some experience. He could usually undo a bra with one hand in the most testing circumstances. He once achieved it with a simple touch on the back of a young lady's blouse at the Sandown Catholic Church Christmas Mass, and only the people in the pew behind noticed. And the young lady, of course. It caused quite a stir at the time, particularly in the front of the young lady's blouse.

Trouble was Tim didn't know her. She was a bit upset, naturally, and so was Tim's girlfriend of-the-time (he had temporarily converted to Catholicism on the strength of the relationship) who was sitting on the other side of him. Tim explained that he was merely dislodging a wasp on the young lady's blouse, but it didn't do much good, given the fact that there aren't that many wasps around at Christmas. And the magistrates refused to consider the fact that he had had 12 pints prior to the service as mitigating circumstances, which was less than generous of them. They gave him a conditional discharge, and said he needed sexual therapy. Charlie offered to come with him, on the assumption that anything to do with sex had to be good.

"But why did you do it?" Charlie asked him after the case.

"Not sure. I suppose it was because they were there. You know, twin peaks, the challenge. That sort of thing."

Anyway, we digress.

Tim and Charlie worked on a flying machine in an old barn up at his dad Arthur's farm. It went very well, for Charlie was pretty good at DIY. He welded together a few lightweight bicycle frames as a fuselage, built some wings out of canvas stretched over wooden supports, and linked a propeller to a bike chain and pedals. "All you have to do is peddle like hell and off you go. The wings will keep you up long enough to gain some momentum, and you should make 50 or 60 yards with no trouble," he had said.

"Why can't you drive it?" Tim replied. It was a daft question, given the fact that Charlie was too tall, and had difficulty squeezing into a telephone box let alone the tiny cockpit he had provided.

"The term is pilot, not driver," he said, impatiently. "I'm not the right shape, but you'll be fine. Anyway, you need me to push you off. We're sure to win."

Charlie had been perfecting the push-off at the local Co-op, by means of loading a supermarket trolley up with beer and sprinting down the aisles with it.

It was unfortunate that Beryl Bloggett, the off-duty traffic warden, happened to turn her trolley into the practice lane at precisely the moment that Charlie hit top speed. There was an almighty crash and Beryl ended up in hospital with whiplash.

"It was a shopping accident," she told a disbelieving nurse. "Our trolleys collided."

"She's confused. She's probably concussed," explained the doctor.

Came the great day. Not everything went to plan. For a start Murphy's lot had borrowed a hang glider, and with the assistance of a stiff off-shore breeze managed to cover about 100 yards before ditching. There was thunderous applause from crowds lining the beach and pier.

"Is that legal?" demanded Charlie. "I thought this competition was supposed to be about designing your own aircraft, not using somebody else's."

It was a good point, because all the other contestants had built their own machines. And a right mess some of them were – wings falling off as they were carried down the pier, pilots jumping straight into the sea and making no attempts to manoeuvre their machines, and a couple of weirdoes who leapt into space beating their arms up and down hoping for a miracle. All were recovered, wet but cheerful, to be welcomed back on to dry land with a handshake from the Mayor.

The organisers conferred, and then the Mayor – chairman of the committee said there was nothing in the rule book to prohibit hang gliders, but they would consider banning them next year.

And so it was the Frog and Trumpet's turn.

Tim didn't have a lot of confidence as he stood there in his bathing trunks, covered in goose pimples, convinced that everyone had their eyes on his assets.

Charlie assisted him onto the seat, secured his feet in the pedal straps and began to push the machine towards the edge of the pier, gaining speed with every stride...

Unfortunately, the competition was running a little late.

It was by now 4pm.... the time that Dare Devil Lester, the masked, drunken one-armed pier diver, performed his daily daredevil feat. This, as any small boy would tell you, largely consisted of threatening spectators with his stump until they placed pennies in a collection box, staggering to the edge of the landing stage and – to the jeers of local urchins falling 30 ft backwards into the water.

It was a miracle he never injured himself.

Dare Devil Lester had forgotten it was the day of the Flying Machine race. Appearing from the lower deck bar, hanging on to the rail for support, he obviously thought the applause was for him. He bowed for the crowd. But then he saw Tim and Charlie and the Flying Pig.

"What's that damn thing?" he demanded. "Get it out of my way."

"Wait until I've taken off," Tim shouted, and started to pedal slowly to get the propeller moving, while the machine rattled forward on its pram wheels.

They carried on with the launch. They went right through the diver. As Tim looked ahead, Lester vanished in a tangle of arm and legs, and then the edge of the pier disappeared from under him. All he could see was the sea.

"We have lift off..." Tim bellowed, peddling like fury. But the words choked in his throat as the machine slowed, its nose dropped and a wing swung wildly around. For the briefest instance he saw the frantic face of the Mayor, framed in a triangle of fuselage and wing strut.

And then he was gone.

Tim didn't know whether he hit the water first, or Lester or the Mayor all he could recollect afterwards was the strong arm of a lifeguard under his shoulders, water in his throat, and the flying machine perched precariously above them, firmly caught on a pier stanchion.

The other newspapers splashed the story. MAYOR SAVED IN DRAMATIC PIER RESCUE screamed the local evening, with a picture of him waving feebly from a stretcher, and Lester – his rescuer– looking proudly on. It was great publicity for the diver, particularly as he had only come upon the Mayor by chance as he swam in his usual one-armed manner in ever-widening circles back towards shore, and the Mayor had grabbed hold of him as he passed.

There was also a picture of Tim as he was helped up a ladder from the sea by a beaming girl lifeguard. It was very embarrassing.

Murphy's lot came round to the Frog and Trumpet to show off their trophy.

"Bit of a flying pig, that machine of yours," one of them said to Charlie, grinning.

"You wait until next year," said Charlie.

Tim thought at the time it was a rash thing to say.

"WHEN I was a youth I did useful things, like picking up bits of wood on the beach, and trainspotting," said Bogey's dad, for the 1000th time. "I was always out in the fresh air. All you ever do is watch TV. It really stinks in your bedroom."

So Bogey and his mate Andrew, who was a bit posh, went trainspotting. The old railway station had been abandoned since the Sandown to Newport line was closed 30 years before. It was due to re-open but right now there was no-one around. They sat on the platform, and Bogey sniffed one of the bottles of the Heaven Scent they had found on the pier.

A scruffy dog barked at them and slunk off. "That's the 60532 Blue Peter, en route to Leeds – immaculate, ain't it?" said Bogey.

"Pure poetry," agreed Andrew.

In the distance, the head of a rabbit popped up and went quickly to earth again.

"Did you see that? It was Black 55305, one of the old steam locos. I just love to see them, don't you?" said Andrew.

"Indeed I do," said his companion, his eyes closed, swirling images of smoke clouding his brain. It made him sneeze, and then he blacked out.

When he woke up, Andrew said: "You were foaming at the mouth and trembling."

Bogey said he was OK.

But for days after he had a recurring dream - the Flying Scotsman was hurtling towards him, as he lay naked on the track, and all he could do was hold one hand out to try and stop it hitting him. The other was around his privates. He woke up sweating and screaming.

"You alright, son?" said his dad, the first time it happened.

"I am, but I'm not going trainspotting again," said Bogey.

CHAPTER 5

"YOU had better wrap up one of those bottles to your uncle, for his birthday. It's the least you can do with all the troubles he's got," said Andrew's mum. She secretly nurtured ambitions that one day Andrew would inherit Sir Humphrey's newspaper empire - and this had been enhanced by her mistaken impression from Lady Dorothy that his virility had made its last.. uh.. stand.

"But mum... I've already given a bottle to Captain Smith, like you asked me. I will be running out of them at this rate."

"No buts. DO it. The poor man... he'll never have a son like you."

Andrew's mum believed in cultivating contacts. She was a friend of the wife of Captain Smith – who operated the ferry out of Sandown Pier – and knew they were childless. Maybe one day, she thought, they would look kindly upon Andrew.

So Andrew graciously handed over one of his Heaven Scent bottles to his uncle. "Thank you, son," said Sir Humphrey. "My pleasure, Sir," replied Andrew, who had been to private school.

That night Lady Dorothy massaged it into Sir Humphrey's scalp. It was a special birthday treat and the prelude to a romp that would have both enlightened and horrified Andrew's mum had she been aware of it, and not tucked up with a hot chocolate and a Barbara Cartland novel.

It was Lady Dorothy who woke first before dawn next morning, and – as was her usual custom – she bent over and planted a kiss on her husband's bald pate, only this time her rosebud lips encountered a shock of unruly hair.

Her scream echoed through the stately corridors of the Potts pile, followed by a dull thud and stream of obscenities.

Housekeeper Dolores Pollypoint, who was in the wash room sorting out Lady Dorothy's old underwear for collection by a charity lady, took the stairs two at a time as she rushed to help.

Lady Potts was on the landing, shaking and ashen-faced, turning a key in the lock of her bedroom door – "There's a strange man in there," she sobbed. "I was dreaming that dear Pottsie and I were making luvvy duvvies, and then when I awoke there was a rascal with long hair beside me. I hit him with a bedside lamp and ran."

"Where's Sir Humphrey?" asked the housekeeper, heading downstairs to the gunroom.

"I don't know. Perhaps he's lying murdered somewhere..."

By the time Mrs Pollypoint returned, someone was kicking at the door from the inside, uttering dire threats of retribution.

"He's pretending to be Pottsie, the swine," said Lady Dorothy. "The nerve of the scoundrel. My poor murdered husband doesn't even know words like that."

Mrs Pollypoint pointed the shotgun at the door.

Lady Dorothy called the police.

Pc Cartwright was on patrol only minutes from Cuckoospit Hall. As his car turned into the drive he could see, in the light of the moon, a long-haired man in striped pyjamas climbing down a drainpipe. The barrel of a shotgun protruded from an upstairs window.

"You beast," shouted Mrs Pollypoint. "Stay where you are or I'll let you have both barrels."

"But it's me, you stupid woman," snarled Sir Humphrey (for it was indeed he), pausing in his descent.

"Who's me?" shouted Pc Cartwright, wishing the shotgun was pointing in the other direction.

"You're Pc Cartwright, fool!" came the impatient reply as Sir Humphrey carried on descending, his fingers raw and cold, his head aching, blood dripping from a wound above his right ear.

"It's not His Lordship," bellowed the defiant Mrs Pollypoint. "His Lordship is a bald gentleman, and this 'ere is an uncouth, long-haired layabout, intent on ravishing her Ladyship... and I'm going to shoot him."

She cocked both barrels of the gun.

"Don't shoot!" cried Sir Humphrey. It was his worst nightmare, struck half-way down a drainpipe, his tackle hanging out of the hole in his pyjamas, being menaced by a crazed servant with a 12-bore. "Don't let her shoot me, Fluffy Rabbit..."

Only dear Rumbletum called her Fluffy Rabbit..

"It IS him. Don't shoot, don't shoot!" screamed Lady Dorothy. She leant out of the window, arms outstretched in recognition, welcoming her husband back to her ample bosom (oh sweet joy, thought Pc Cartwright, hypnotised by their magnificent protuberance).

It was unfortunate that in her exuberance, Fluffy Rabbit knocked Mrs Pollypoint's trigger finger. There were two mighty bangs as the shotgun went off.

It is with regret that it must be reported that Traffic Warden Beryl Bloggett, who had been on her way to a traffic warden convention in Ventnor, in responding to the emergency-all-vehicles call from police HQ, chose to arrive in her three-wheeler at precisely that moment. Whilst Mrs Pollypoint's first shot merely grazed the drainpipe above Sir Humphrey's head, sending him tumbling in an untidy heap to the flower bed below, her second scored a direct hit on Miss Bloggett's windscreen.

Though the good woman was not physically hurt. she was so shocked she completely lost her rattle, abandoning the wheel to fate whilst pressing her foot hard down on the accelerator. Fortunately the ornamental fishpond was not very deep.

Pc Cartwright waded out to coax her from the vehicle by promising her she could blow his whistle. "She's a complete nut case," said Sir Humphrey uncharitably as she sat next to him in the ambulance, whimpering and sucking his thumb.

They kept her in hospital. Sir Humphrey was released after a check-up.

"They don't know why I grew so much hair grew so quickly. It's like a miracle. Maybe it had something to do with young Andrew's after-shave, but who cares," he confided to his wife. "I reckon it's taken 20 years off me...."

"Now you're my little hairy Rumbletum," said Lady Dorothy, running her fingers through his curls. Strangely, the hair had a slight greenish tint, but she never mentioned it. She gently kissed the plaster covering the wound where she had bashed him.

AND then life returned to normal for a few days, apart from the arrival of the anti-terrorist squad from Scotland Yard, a team of hard-faced men who spoke with the same London accent as Harry, and were soon turning up at local pubs and clubs trying to look casual and inconspicuous as they listened in on conversations and whispered in corners.

Charlie noticed them as he sat at the bar in the Royal Oak, and they noticed him.

"See that chap talking to the barmaid, the one with the spots?" said one heavy to his mate.

"What barmaid with spots?" said his mate, who was not terribly quick.

"No, she hasn't got the spots, it's him."

"Why has he got spots?"

"I don't care why he has them. It's irreverent. Anyway, I saw him snooping around the police station earlier. We will have to watch him."

"I've got spots. It doesn't do you any good with women," said his mate, sympathetically.

King Alfred the chef had been busy in the Chronicle. The canteen sausages were ruined. They were stiff as board, and charred black around the edges. "You could use them to shore up the pier," Tim pointed out.

"I will probably end up giving the lot to Charlie's dad, Arthur," said Edna, who served behind the counter.

Arthur was a daily caller at the Chronicle and many other parts of the town, collecting food scraps for his pig farm. He was an amputee, which Charlie said was an old war wound, and wore a false leg.

When Charlie wasn't working or unsuccessfully trying to chat up barmaids, he often went round to the farm to see his dad. He loved the farm. It was peaceful. He would walk inside the farmhouse and chill out – you know, fart, and spit in the fire. The usual thing. Like father, like son. The hot tiles around the fireplace were spattered with spit marks where they had missed. Sizzling spit.

If his dad wasn't home, he would stand outside and watch the pigs, snouts down in mud, snorting, rubbing their bottoms against the railings. They fascinated him. The pigs watched Charlie picking his nose and scratching his groin. He fascinated them.

Charlie was broke as usual, driving his 12-year-old Anglia without MOT or road tax. He was always on the lookout for a woman, someone who wouldn't mind his poverty, who liked him as he was, smart new beard, booze and all.

"It must be nice to be promiscuous," he sighed to his dad one evening.

"Bit too energetic when you've got one leg," observed Arthur.

"I wouldn't mind just being a little bit promiscuous, you know every now and again, or even once a month, after all it is supposed to be the permissive society."

"Difficult to get your leg over," said Arthur, contemplating his stump.

"I mean, it's not really permissive if not everyone is doing it, is it? It's wrongly named, gives the wrong impression. People might think, looking at me, that I must be one of them promiscuous people but I'm not. It's not fair, really, is it! You get the wrong reputation and you haven't had any of the fun."

"I'd be going at it half-cocked," said Arthur, giggling at his own joke.

"Anyway, I'd better go," said Charlie. "Thanks for the chat, it helps to tell someone your little problems."

"I'm a good listener," agreed his dad.

＼

CHAPTER 6

THERE were only five on the Chronicle editorial staff, Charlie and Tim, Millie who did the women's page and features, old Phil the sub and planner, and Greg the photographer.

Phil sat at his desk and bored for Britain. He would rant and rave about any unfortunate soul that crossed his path, from poor old Beryl Bloggett – "She booked me just because I was in a disabled parking area. Bloody disabled! Half of them are as fit as I am" – to the doctor who examined his wife – "She had to wait half an hour, and then he said there was nothing wrong with her! Complete waste of time. If he said that to me, I'd drop him!" – and the state of the country – "The arrogant toads, they're not interested in the working man."

But even that was mildly interesting compared to his tales from the riverbank, and deep-sea fishing adventures off the Needles. Milly became so used to pretending to listen, and making vague responses, that she was woken by a phone call from Phil one Sunday morning at 7am and discovered she had agreed to go eel fishing in the Hamble estuary. She was too nice to turn him down, but said later it was the most miserable day of her life.

Phil never took his wife fishing. She was hugely relieved that he had never asked her; it was out of character because he totally controlled her life.

Phil slammed the phone down. "Why doesn't she answer?" he moaned. He phoned long-suffering Maud every half-hour to find out what she was doing.

"Maybe she's on the loo?" suggested Tim.

"Or gone out with a friend?" stirred Charlie.

"Friend, what friend? She hasn't any friends. Who are you talking about?" asked Phil suspiciously.

"Nothing, but she's an attractive woman...."

Phil was already back on the phone. There was no answer. So he tried again, and again....

Life was tedious. They had no contact with the editor, who sat in his office and arranged lunches with business people, and had no idea which stories went in the paper.

"What we need is another bomb," said Greg, gazing hopefully out over the roofs of the town.

"I know where I'd put it, or rather I know who I'd put it under," said Charlie.

"We're a ship without a rudder. Full steam ahead, and the captain's in Cuckoo Land," said Tim.

CAPTAIN Nathaniel Smith was drunk. He stood in his cabin on the Sandown Queen tanked up to the eyeballs with best bitter and double whiskies, and longed for another drink. The mate was at the controls on the bridge, and there were, at best, only about a dozen passengers on board. Next stop Southsea.

He fumbled for a mirror. A greying scalp, blotchy, wrinkled face, wispy moustache and blood-flecked eyes, deeply shadowed, peered back at him. He had picked up a photo of the wife by mistake.

It would soon be his 40th wedding anniversary. I'll drink to that, he thought. But there was nothing to drink.

A bottle of green after-shave stood on the table. He had almost forgotten it. That young lad, what was his name, Andrew, had given it to him. What a nice lad. Wonder if it's got alcohol in it?

It said Heaven Scent in large, badly printed letters, and underneath the warning "Do Not Shake." He pulled the cap off and sniffed. It smelt like green pears and the skin of dark-haired girls on a wet beach at midnight. It reminded him of clear Mediterranean waters, swimming up between the firm, moist thighs of his first love. He ached with a passion he thought long dead.

It tasted slightly bitter. Nathaniel gave it a vigorous shake. It foamed up and made weird popping noises. After a moment or two, he took another swig.

There was a slight after-burn, but on the whole it was very pleasant. Cleared his head. Everything suddenly came into focus. Dear Edna's sweet face. The grubby white cover on his peaked cap. The thick, green toenail protruding through a hole in his socks.

He felt very content and philosophical. I will share this moment with the crew and passengers, thought he. After I've broken wind.

His stomach had suddenly started to churn. Pheeeeeart. Pheeeeeeaaaart. Pheeeeeeeeartaartaaartaart.

Phew!

He left his cabin and wandered past the nearly empty cafeteria. A few passengers were huddled in the middle, trying to ignore the ship's movement.

Pheeuuuurt! Pheeeeuuuaaaart! Pheeethwaaaaaart!

Beryl Bloggett was day-dreaming. She was quite used to ferry travel, because she took the Sandown Queen every week to see her mother in Southsea. Her painful left arm, injured in the road accident near the cliffs the previous week, was at last feeling better. The motion of the sea didn't upset her, it fact it may even have stimulated her fantasy. She was rocking gently on a hammock, amongst palm trees, surrounded by white sand, the sun on her back and a handsome, dark young man massaging oil into the muscle on her left thigh.

It was the smell that brought her back to reality. A dreadful, clinging, stink that came out of nowhere, like liquefied excrement from a farmer's muck spreader, or something altogether more sinister, gangrenous flesh or death itself.

And then Captain Smith appeared amongst the passengers. His eyes were glazed and he was almost incoherent. "Are you all all-right, all of you?" he said, with an all-embracing sweep of his arm that upset his balance and carried him across to the other side of the cafeteria. Phwoaroaroarararaaaaaart!

Green fumes appeared from the bottom of his trousers. Beryl fumbled for a handkerchief, holding it over her nose as she attempted to move past the swaying old salt towards the door. She desperately needed fresh air.

"You're that traffic warden lady, aren't you?" croaked captain Smith, peering closely at her. "Well, you can't give me a ticket, 'cos I'm not standing still." And he laughed so much his body went into a spin and pirouetted wildly across the floor, cutting a swathe through the tables and chairs, sending passengers sprawling. Pheeeeeeeeeeeeeeewaaaaaaaaaaaaaoaoaoaggggggg! Pheeeooooowwwwoggg!

More clouds of noxious green fumes bulged their way down his trousers. People fled in all directions.

On the bridge the first mate could hear people shouting, but did not understand why until the sliding door was pulled back and strands of green mist came pulsing in, getting thicker by the second, accompanied by an awful stench. It was like something out of The Fog, only worse. Through the cloud he could just make out the figure of the captain.

Old Smith was in a terrible state. His stomach was giving him great pain, and his wits were befuddled. "I need a drink, I need a drink," he muttered, clutching the mate by the shoulders.

"Get orf, get orf, I can't see where we are going!"

"Give us a drink, old friend. Just to toast the wife. Married 40 years we are, and she still doesn't know her port from her starboard."

The mate couldn't stand the fumes any more. His eyes were stinging and chest wheezing, He pushed the captain away and ran out into the fresh air.

"I know, " said Captain Smith, to himself, "I'll have another drink of that Heaven Scent stuff in my cabin."

And he left the bridge in a concerto of farts - Pheeee! Phruuurp! Thruuuurrraaaaaaaaaaarrrrrrrrrrrrrrppppp!

IT was Pc Cartwright who drew Blunder's attention to the strange events unfolding at sea. A huge cloud of green fumes had appeared over the Sandown Queen which had stopped about 300 yards from the pier head, and appeared to be drifting closer.

Blunder grabbed the binoculars. "There's a few people running around on the deck. I can see two or three jumping into the sea. Quick, call the police!"

The constable had the telephone to his ear before he realised what he was doing. – "But we are the police..."

"Oh, yes, well, get the fire brigade," ordered Blunder.

A few office blocks away in the Chronicle newsroom, Tim was typing out a golden wedding report when young Greg dashed past, clutching his camera. "There's something going on in Sandown Bay," he shouted.

At that moment there was a mighty explosion. From the window they could see a pall of greeny-black smoke near the pier, and, as it cleared, the Sandown Queen, listing heavily to port (or was it starboard?). Someone was trying to lower a boat from the side, and a few heads were bobbing about in the water.

"It's another bomb," shouted Greg gleefully.

"Tory bastards," said Phil, putting the phone down on his wife.

The editorial team beat the police to the beach by five minutes. They borrowed a rowing boat and put their weight behind the oars. As they approached the survivors, Greg taking photos as quickly as he could, Tim could see Pc Cartwright still on the shore attempting to start the police boat's outboard motor.

The mist had cleared. The Sandown Queen had collided with the pier and tilted over, but did not appear to be sinking. A large, ragged hole ran down the side of the ship from just behind the shattered bridge to water level. A curtain flapped in the wind.

Charlie and Tim helped a woman and little boy off a rope ladder into the boat, both too exhausted to say anything. Tim saw an arm waving feebly, before it vanished below the surface. He dived in.

"I don't know why, because I am not a good swimmer," he said later, in an exclusive interview with the Chronicle. "But you do, don't you."

It was pure luck that, in his blind panic, striking out desperately towards the shore, his arm struck an object, and that object turned out to be a woman. The shock of it brought him back to reality. His throat was full of sea water as he kicked and spat his way back to the rowing boat, towing her by the hair.

Charlie knew some first-aid. As Tim and Greg rowed back to the beach he gave her the kiss of life. She started breathing again, and as soon as they hit the shingle a bogus doctor ran forward and started to massage her chest. Charlie pulled him away and sat on him.

An ambulance arrived and the young woman was rushed off. The bogus doctor was arrested.

They all sat exhausted on a seat on the esplanade.

Survivors, wrapped in blankets, were helped to a fleet of ambulances. "That's that traffic warden woman," said Charlie, as they carried Beryl Bloggett past on a stretcher, her peaked cap askew, an oxygen mask covering her face. A man in uniform, who Charlie said was the First Mate, walked past and clambered unaided into the ambulance.

A few yards off the beach Supt Blunder stood issuing orders like Nelson at Trafalgar, trying to instill some enthusiasm into Pc Cartwright who sat sullenly at the oars. They were adrift in the police motor boat which had briefly kicked into life before back-firing noisily, and giving up completely.

"TIM was the hero, more than me," said Charlie, graciously.

They were sitting on a fence at Arthur's farm. The old man hadn't said a lot but Charlie knew how proud he was.

"Poor old Nathaniel," muttered Arthur.

The Chronicle had, of course, been full of the story, with page after page of exclusive interviews and pictures (although Greg had discreetly sold some of the best ones to the national papers).

It was nice to be noticed. And they were both glad to have saved the young woman. Her name was Jemma, and although she was still in hospital the word was that she would be leaving soon. Charlie said they should go and see her.

Tim felt a bit awkward. He couldn't remember much about the actual rescue, apart from being cold and scared, really scared. And then there were her breasts. He didn't want to look, but he did. She was half dead, wet and bedraggled, lying there in the boat, and her blouse was stretched tight and transparent. He felt terrible as soon as he'd looked at them. And he still felt guilty. It was an intrusion into her privacy. My God, what sort of sexual pervert was he? That's why he covered her with his coat, even though that was soaked through and heavy as lead.

They hadn't found the captain's body, just a blood-soaked shoe. Police frogmen had searched around the pier without success. The Sandown Queen, taken under tow by tugs, was being examined in dry dock by members of the bomb squad. Blunder, their spokesman, had no doubt this was another terrorist bomb attack, possibly by the IRA. The press had raised the question of the green smoke, and Captain Smith's peculiar behaviour, but Blunder played it all down. "Hysterical witnesses," he said.

Today was Tim's day off. He and Smithy had gone for a long walk. The dog chased rabbits and was in turn chased by some cows. He came hurtling through a thick hedge, so fast the thorns didn't have time to scratch him. Smithy herded some geese and had a good roll in their droppings. They ended up at the farm because it was full of interesting smells for the dog, which poked his nose into everything and regularly had it scratched by cats and pecked by chicken, but patiently put up with it. He never chased them. He and old Arthur, who gave him chicken pellets to eat as a reward, seemed to have an understanding.

Tim found it quite restful to sit and watch Polly, Arthur's prize sow. Sometimes she lay still, her huge flanks shuddering, blissfully asleep despite the squabbling piglets that fought to get at her teats. But as soon as Arthur switched on his compressed air pump, setting pipes rattling noisily through the roof of ramshackle tin sheds, she would stagger to her feet and gamble about the pen, impatient to be fed.

Arthur collected waste food from restaurants and hotels in the town, boiled it all up and pumped it out along the pipes to the pig pens. If a pig was a bit slow waking up it would get a squirt of boiling condensed pork pie, beefburger, pork scratching, beetroot and ice cream in the ear.

Polly was up to her eyebrows in the stuff, if pigs have eyebrows. Tim couldn't really see because she was wearing a fringe of congealed tomato sauce and custard. She had a blackened sausage roll, which looked strangely familiar, adhering to the top of her head. Very fashionable.

"Splendid knockers," observed Charlie, who had a feel for these sorts of things.

"She should have, raising all these little ones," said his dad, proudly.

CHAPTER 7

THE anti-terrorist squad had been on observation outside the Chronicle office for over an hour. Six were pretending to be gasmen. They wore identical police issue gas fitter overalls, and those annoying peaked caps that young people wear rebelliously back-to-front. Superintendent Blunder was there as an adviser, wearing the same blue overalls and cap but also dark glasses, so they knew he was important.

One man was camouflaged as a High Street preacher, shabby trousers and coat and (strangely) a large bishop's mitre. He was carrying a large banner that proclaimed "God has Room for YOU in his Kingdom" and trying to hand out religious leaflets to passers by.

Charlie and Tim watched him from their office window.

"He's not the usual preacher, he's a lot younger," said Tim.

"Maybe he's the son of God," said Charlie irreverently.

The bible pusher's presence was largely ignored by passers-by until another, older man arrived carrying a similar large banner which proclaimed "There is Only One God and he forgives Sinners."

"That's God," said Charlie.

The late arrival took issue with the young pretender.

"This is my pitch. Bugger off," he proclaimed.

"Sod you, I was here first," said the undercover cop.

"There's not room for both of us, and I've always been here," said the real preacher.

"The Kingdom of God has room for everyone," said the cop, pointing at his slogan. He was becoming a bit too involved in his role.

"Not here it doesn't," said his rival, with which he thwacked the policeman across the head with his banner.

In seconds an unseemly brawl broke out between the two men, banners and fists in all directions, and wild oaths that made mothers and passing journalists cover the ears of small children and hurry quickly on.

It ended when three 'gas men' hauled their colleague off his opponent and held him in a darkened doorway until he cooled off.

"I'm not sure what came over me. It was like a shining light around me, suddenly extinguished by a dark cloud," he muttered, still clutching his banner.

"That must have been when he rammed that stupid hat over your eyes," said a colleague.

Blunder tried to concentrate on movements in and out of the newspaper office. He was convinced Charlie had something to do with the bombings.

"When he comes out, stick to him. He'll lead us to the explosives," he told Pc Cartwright, who had been seconded to the squad with a police dog. Brutus was in a police van, parked on a back street.

The constable was not so sure. He knew Charlie from way back.

"Why do you suspect him?" he asked.

"Born trouble maker. Seen them before. Hairy eyebrows."

"But you can't judge a man just because of his eyebrows!"

"It's more than that, of course," said Blunder. "O'Flaherty has been in trouble before, minor stuff maybe, but the seeds of terrorism are there. And, of course, he has an Irish name. He's an obvious suspect. He was too quickly on the scene when the car blew up, and with the ferry."

So would we have been, thought Pc Cartwright, had it not been for your cock-ups.

"And now he's started wearing a false beard," continued the Superintendent.

Pc Cartwright was stunned. Charlie, in disguise? Maybe he was involved, after all.

It started to drizzle. The undercover squad stayed undercover in a fancy red and white striped tent over a hole they'd dug in the road, taking turns to sit in the hole and bang old pipes together to make it sound as if they were working, like gas fitters do everywhere.

It was a dangerous spot. The High Street had been turned into a "Buses Only" zone several months before and for the drivers the novelty of driving as fast as they could along the empty road, causing pedestrians to leap for their lives, before screeching to a halt inches from terrified old folk on the zebra crossing, had not worn off.

Charlie and Tim sat in the bay window of the Frog and Trumpet and watched the police. They had escaped unobserved from the office out of the Chronicle's loading bay. Daphne had a couple of pints waiting.

"What a load of plonkers," Tim said. "They obviously think it's something to do with us."

"Can't think why, but they are hot on the scent of something," Charlie agreed.

It was getting dark. There was no sign of them giving up their vigil.

Daphne hovered.

"I like that perfume you're wearing, Charlie," she said at last, bosoms heaving. "All spicy, and sunshiny. Quite turns me on. And that beard really suits you."

Charlie beamed at her. It wasn't often that a girl made a fuss of him. In fact, never.

"Thanks. It's after-shave. I got it off that lad Andrew, old Potts's nephew. Poured some on my socks. They were a bit whiffy."

"You certainly have style," said she, and she winked at Tim.

Charlie's growth of beard had been quite dramatic, from skin as smooth as Daphne's inner thigh to a full Rasputin job in two days.

"It must be something to do with my virility," he explained, proudly. "No sooner had I shaved that it started to grow again, so I decided not to bother. Reckon I must have suddenly developed more male hormones than most."

"You're a very macho guy," Tim agreed, winking back at Daphne.

"Weird thing is that my hair chest is growing fast, as well. And it's a weird colour, slightly green. Glows a bit in the dark."

"Green for 'Go'? Maybe it should be red for danger," teased Daphne.

"I saw some blond Swedish girls on the esplanade," volunteered Tim, sensing that Daphne might be more interested in him.

Charlie loved Swedish girls, who visited the town every summer. They were confident and sensual and liked sex, or so he had heard. One girl last summer had taught him to say "Mina byxor är på brand," which, she said, meant "I love you." But he hadn't had a chance to try it out. Maybe tonight, with his new beard, they would find him particularly sexy.

He decided to try his luck in the bars on the esplanade. He left by the back door to avoid Blunder's gang.

Daphne came round to Tim's side of the bar. They were alone. She bought him a pint and gave herself a double gin, and then went and locked the bar doors. "It's more intimate," she giggled.

"Where's Harry tonight?" he said nervously.

"I don't know, nor care. He's changed. Don't see so much of him, and when I do he's aggressive."

She undid the top buttons on her blouse. "This is what he did to me."

There was a large black and red bruise at the top of her arm.

"Why?" Tim said, lamely.

He was feeling a little anxious, not sure how to handle the situation. This was, after all, Daphne. She had been Harry's woman as long as he had known her.

"Why? He doesn't need a reason. He just likes to dominate people. There's another on this arm, and ... well, look at this."

She pulled over the shoulder strap on her other shoulder, and pulled the bra down a few centimetres. It had started as a love bite, but got out of hand, she said. The skin was torn and bloody. These were teeth marks.

"I've had enough of him, Tim. And he seems to have lost interest as well, apart from the sex. I've been wondering if he had somebody else."

She was weeping. Her blouse was open; her bra had slipped down even further.

Tim put an arm around her shoulders, and she buried her face in his chest.

"What about your husband? Hasn't he noticed the bruises?"

"He's got his bits on the side. He's not bothered about me."

Her face was close, the scent overpowering. "I always liked you Tim," she said.

"Do you like dogs?" he asked hopefully.

"Not much, but let's not think about that. Now you have done something for me, I want to reward you."

She kissed his neck, and her tongue started to explore his right ear.

"Done what?" he wasn't really bothered, given the situation that was developing, but had to ask.

"My sister, Jemma. You saved her. She was the girl on the Sandown Queen... "

As far as Tim was concerned, at that moment, she might just as well have been the Queen of Sheba. He had more pressing things on his mind.

We should draw a discreet veil over the events that unfolded, but owe it to the plot to reveal the extent to which their relationship then developed. Tim did not, as one is supposed to do in the spirit of decent journalism, make an excuse and leave.

CHAPTER 8

YOUNG Andrew Potts nervously examined his hair. He had arranged to meet Angela Braithwaite on the beach for a midnight swim. Angela was also 15, but a lot more street-wise than he was. He didn't usually mix in her circles. She thought he was very proper but she liked his private-school manner. In a rash moment he boasted to her that he regularly skinny-dipped near the pier at night. "What even in winter?" said she. "Indeed I do," said he. "Then I'll come with you on Friday night," she said. Angela was game for anything.

Which is how Andrew got his awful hair cut.

"I reckon she might," said Bogey.

"Might what?" said Andrew, not knowing much about that sort of thing.

"You know, do it," said Bogey.

"Then I'd better get a condom," said Andrew; as if it was something he did every day.

He nipped into the men's toilet at the Frog and Trumpet but the machine was empty (the landlord was away for a few days, and had taken the lot). So Andrew called in at the Red Lion (the condom machine was broken), the White Horse (three Hell's Angels were heaving the machine through the loo window) and the Jolly Sailor (he put in four pounds and all that came out was a Kit Kat.)

So Andrew tried Boots the chemists. He hovered nervously for several minutes, trying to look interested in headache tablets and bandages. Then he moved on, only to find himself gazing at the Tampon shelves. He plucked up the nerve to pick up a pack of Durex Ribbed For Extra Sensitivity, and approached the counter. The assistant was young and pretty. "Packet of throat sweets, please," he said, trying to hide the condoms. She had to go all the way down the other end of the shop to get them. They both blushed. He put the condoms back where he had found them.

Mick the barber was the last resort. He was an old-fashioned men's hairdresser who charged a few bob for a trim all round and sold something for the weekend. Andrew had his haircut and was just about to ask for a packet of rubbers when a voice behind him said: "How's your mum, Andrew?" It was old Derek 'Oooti-Tooti', the Vicar.

So he went back next day. He steadied himself for the ordeal, leant on the door handle and pushed, Nothing happened. Maybe it's closed, he thought, panicking. His date was that evening. But there were people inside, so he put his shoulder against the door and it swung open with a crash, catapulting him across the floor.

"Stuck, were it?" said Mick, without turning his head. Snip, snip.

Andrew decided to hang around until the place was empty. Bogey's dad came in after him, but Andrew said he was in no hurry and let him go first.

When it was his turn, Mick said: "You back again? Want some stuck back?"

"Cut it shorter please."

And he did.

And so it was that Andrew turned up on the beach late that evening wearing a woolly hat, with one of Mick's blackcurrant flavoured "rubber rib ticklers" burning a hole in his pocket,

Angela reached out from between two beach huts and pulled him in. They kissed breathlessly, their tongues twisting and thrusting like eels trapped in a jam jar.

"Where's your swimming trunks?" said Angela.

"I'm wearing them."

"So am I," she giggled.

They started to disrobe. "Blooming cold," he said, hoping she'd take the hint.

"Aren't you going to take that silly hat off?"

He did. She ran off across the sand, with Andrew in pursuit, yelling Indian war cries, straight into the surf.

It was surprisingly light, splashing around between the breakers. The drizzle had stopped and the stars were out. When Angela had had enough they ran back to the shelter of the beach huts, towelling themselves vigorously and leaping about to keep warm. They sat side by side, draped in towels. A shaft of light from a street lamp illuminated her face.

"You've got lovely blue eyes," he said.

"Thanks....." She quite liked him. "You smell strange, like bruised bananas. What is it?"

"It's my after–shave. Heaven Scent it's called."

"Nice. And I like your stubble. Very manly. But your hair cut is awful."

Andrew's stubble had materialised almost overnight. He had meant to shave it off, but hadn't got a razor.

Angela fondled his chin.

He felt overwhelmed by the warm, wet near nakedness of her. In that magic moment as his lips reached out for hers he noticed a tiny white pimple on the end of her nose. He loved her for it – it was a flaw against the pale silk of her skin, but only as a pearl is a blemish in the flesh of an oyster. He felt like kissing away the angry flush that surrounded it.

"What are you gawping at?" asked Angela, pulled away, mistaking his motives.

"Nothing..."

"Yes you are, it's only a rotten spot, Stop peering at it."

They sat in silence for a moment. He moved a little closer. She did not resist. They kissed, frantically. While she was distracted, he used a foot to manoeuvre his trousers nearer, and felt to make sure the condom was still secure in his pocket. It wasn't. The contraceptive packet fell out on the sand just as she surfaced for air.

Angela looked at it, and stood up in disgust – "You must be kidding!" she said. "I thought you were different to the others."

It took just a few moments to pull her jeans and coat on over her wet swimsuit, pack up the towel and storm off across the beach. Andrew sat and watched her go. It was just his luck. No doubt everyone would be laughing at him when word got around.

It was really depressing being a figure of fun.

The incident with the elephant hadn't helped. It had happened last summer. He had taken a neighbour's little boy to Sandown Zoo. The little lad wanted a ride on an elephant. The elephant knelt and they were helped up onto a platform on its back. The elephant walked round in a circle several times, and for some reason a large crowd gathered. They were all laughing.

Some of his friends were there, pointing and giggling so much one of them fell off a wall. Andrew imagined they must be laughing at him. Perhaps, he thought wildly, he was too old to go on an elephant.

What he didn't know until he got off was that suddenly and inexplicably the elephant, renowned for its lethargy, had developed an eight-foot erection. Poor Andrew! He felt so humiliated that he wouldn't go out for two days.

Nor would the elephant.

Oh well, better get home, he thought. He pulled his shirt on and wriggled out of his trunks, and was just bending over to pick up his underpants when something blew a wet raspberry on his bare bottom. No, it wasn't Angela, mores the pity. The largest dog he had ever seen was pushing frantically at his posterior, frothing at the mouth, making strange choking noises.

And then out of the gloom a voice said: "Don't move, this is the police. One word from me and Brutus will tear you apart."

Pc Cartwright appeared.

"Oh, it's you," they each said, in unison. They knew one another through Bogey's dad.

Pc Cartwright, however – feeling particularly brave because he had charge of a police dog – was determined to do his duty.

"I have reason to believe that you have explosives concealed about your person," he said.

"Hardly likely, as I haven't got any clothes on, " replied the lad.

"This dog is highly trained to detect explosive substances," said Pc Cartwright. "It can sniff out drugs in a sewage farm and bombs in a manure heap."

"If you ask me it's perverted," said Andrew, trying to hold the beast's cold nose back from his privates.

Pc Cartwright called for assistance.

The anti-terrorist squad were considerably relieved to get his call. The gas van hurtled down to the esplanade, it's anonymity spoilt by the fact that a blue light flashed on top and a work experience policeman was making siren noises through his nose. It considerably annoyed his colleagues.

Seven officers shone torches down at Pc Cartwright and Andrew. The dog was now dribbling over Andrew's shoulder bag.

"Throw down your weapon," shouted Blunder dramatically.

"Don't be silly," said Andrew. The poor lad was still wearing only his shirt, and was shivering with cold.

"Search the bag," ordered the Superintendent.

The young policeman carefully unzipped the bag and used a stick to pull out the contents. He lifted a pair of yellow and red spotted underpants towards the policemen above. No-one was in a hurry to take them.

There was a watch, and some keys and a bottle of after-shave. Nothing suspicious. Andrew put them back.

They allowed Andrew to dress. As he did so, Pc Cartwright carried the bag to the van. It was evidence. He threw it in the back.

There was a massive explosion. A vivid green flash lit up the sky over Sandown, followed by a tremendous bang and rush of air.

Andrew was knocked flat on the sand. He examined himself carefully in case anything undercover was missing, though he doubted he would ever use it.

Seven undercover police caps floated gently down into the sea. A wheel rolled crazily along the beach, crushing a pair of dark glasses at the water's edge.

Supt Blunder sat up and pushed aside a young person's legs. He wished he would stop making siren noises. Crumpled bodies lay all around.

Miraculously, Pc Cartwright was the only one standing. The police dog cowered in his arms.

The police van had virtually disintegrated. A blue light flickered drunkenly on top of the statue of Ernest O'Flaherty.

They briefly detained Andrew, but it was obvious he had nothing to do with the blast.

They arrested Charlie as he lurched past on his way to his fifth pub of the evening. He had tried his luck with another Swedish girl student only to discover that his words of love meant, in fact, "my trousers are on fire." The girl couldn't stop giggling and none of her friends would take him seriously after that.

Charlie was completely oblivious to the fact that there had been another explosion, "What bomb?" he said, wading knee-deep in bent metal and burnt rubber, before falling headlong on top of that luckless traffic warden Beryl Bloggett, who was curled up on a stretcher awaiting transport back to hospital suffering shock and minor lacerations having been felled by a flying number plate as she left a nearby chippie (some might say that was poetic justice).

Pc Cartwright tried unsuccessfully to interrogate Charlie, who kept falling asleep. The officer gave his beard a sharp tug just to see if it was real. It was. The reporter slept on. They held him in a cell overnight, searched his house, and found nothing.

A strange luminous substance had been discovered on the spare wheel of the shattered police van, which would in time be analysed by Forensics, but they were currently three weeks behind with all their investigations, having lost staff due to privatisation. It was now run by a security company which also ran a local prison and had eyes on the police service itself. Attempts to match the liquid with previous explosions and Charlie's clothes would have to wait.

In the morning he was cautioned for being drunk and disorderly and released. A plain clothes bobby, in police-issue torn jeans, black imitation-leather jacket and sensible shoes, followed a discreet distance behind as he headed for the office.

ANDREW was worried. He held a bottle of Heaven Scent carefully in the palm of his hand, and sniffed the top. "It's a strange mixture alright – it keeps making popping noises, and it glows in the dark," he said.

Bogey nodded agreement,

"It's weird. I put some on my chin and next morning there were so many hairs I had to shave again. Second time in a month," he said,

"I stopped using it," said Andrew. "It smelt nice but it was like rubbing bleach into your skin – it stung like mad, and made my face go numb. So I gave some to my uncle."

"What, old Pottsie?"

"Yep. And you know how bald he is, well, he's been rubbing it into his head and his hair has started to grow again. He reckons it's wonderful."

They had two bottles left in their possession.

"How many did we leave in the pier pavilion?" asked Andrew.

"Three, I think. I remember there were about ten in all."

"Do you think this stuff is causing the explosions?" said Andrew.

"It can't be. It's only after-shave."

"We don't know that. The fact is that each time something has blown up, there's been a bottle of Heaven Scent involved. It can't be co-incidence, there must be a link."

"My girlfriend says it smells really good," said Bogey defiantly. "She gets all passionate when I've got it on."

"Well, I'm sorry, but I think we ought to either tell the police or do something about it ourselves. Smash them up, perhaps. It's the decent thing to do."

"We could smash that one, and see what happens," said Bogey.

So they went to the field behind Arthur O'Flaherty's pig farm and placed the bottle in the largest cowpat they could find – it was about three hours old, Bogey reckoned. He had earned a Boy Scout badge for tracking cows before he discovered that following girls was more fun.

The cowpat was soft and wet under a crunchy top, and the bottle settled in firmly.

Then they retired behind the shelter of a hedge and lobbed half bricks at it.

After about five throws each, Andrew hit the target ....

It was more of a WHOOSH! than a BANG! A flash of green light, a blast of hot air that knocked the lads flat and singed their extremities, and a blackened hole three metres in diameter where the cowpat had been.

CHAPTER 9

ABOUT 80 miles above the Isle of Wight, Russian Army Colonel Alexander Buchov was trying to carry out a manoeuvre that anywhere else might have been recognised as beyond the call of duty. Assisting him was United States Navy Lieutenant Anastasia Power, bleeding profusely from a wound above her right eyebrow.

She was a pretty girl, in a barbie-doll sort of way. Perfect teeth, lovely smile, cosmetic bust. She was also a good scientist and technician, and reasonably fit, which is how she came to be partnering cosmonaut Colonel Buchov on a 12 month US-Russia assignment aboard the space station MIR III.

Buchov was a hunky Rusky – tall, with a muscular, hairy body. If he had a preference as far as women were concerned, it was for more homely girls than Annie. But he was not into women much anyway, preferring to spend his evenings in the company of a thick, massively technical book on astro-engineering.

He had been putting off his close encounter with Miss Power for some time, but at last, fortified by vodka, he set about it in determined fashion.

It was with the ultimate goal of sending cosmonauts on long voyages of exploration into space, and perhaps for space settlers to spend their lives in controlled environment 'bubbles' on the surface of far-off planets, that the Human Biology Unit at Moscow University and the Institute of Human Resource in Washington decided to examine the effects of weightlessness on the human procreation process, ie making and having babies in a vacuum.

It was felt that a joint exercise would be of immense value to international relations in the new spirit of Glasnost, even though it was to be kept secret in case anything went wrong.

And so it was that Col Buchov and his partner, both naked from the waist down, were there above Sandown, grappling frantically for each other to the sound of the Beatles' latest hit Yesterday – which was a sell-out in Moscow – as they floated around the chamber prior to penetration.

Twice they had collided, propelling Anastasia backwards, spinning wildly out of control. She had banged her head on a button on the control panel (it switched on an interior video camera that transmitted their contortions to a stunned control room in Vladivostoc) and she was getting fed up with the whole idea.

"Let's try again," said the Colonel, focussing his mind on the centrefold of a Christmas edition of Electronical Engineer magazine (a particularly erotic plan of a new robotic oil drilling system) clipped to the desk below him. Lieut Power breast-stroked her way back to his side; they bumped, squirmed for a moment, and were suddenly coupled together, gasping.

"Contact!" shouted a dozen excited voices in Vladivostok, although of course the cosmonauts didn't hear them.

It may not have been the start of a beautiful relationship, but it would have been a triumph for science had not at that very moment the space station began to rock wildly from side to side, hurling papers, clothes and delicate machinery across the living quarters, and detaching the Colonel's rampaging penis from its anchor point between his companion's silken thighs.

"We have separation," observed the officer of the watch in Vladivostok Control. "Aaah, separation," groaned the international observers.

The couple flew apart, the Colonel bruising his privates on the corner of the liquid food dispenser and poor Anastasia ending upside down behind the human waste disposal unit, under the unblinking gaze of the video camera, her modesty destroyed for ever.

"Vot 'vos that?" shouted General Von Schweinhund at Mission Control. Once a famous German space pioneer, he was now – a sprightly octogenarian – head of the Russian space programme.

"Sudden rush of propulsion from below," reported Colonel Buchov, nursing his injured member. "It's ruined the experiment and damaged my equipment."

"Is your performance compromised?"

"Well, I don't know until I try it again. It's feeling very bruised."

Von Schweinhund snorted, exasperated. "Not that, idiot. The way the space station operates. Are you maintaining orbit? Is there any oxygen loss? Can you continue your duties?"

The Colonel put his trousers on, turned Lieut Power the right way up and inspected her monitors. They were OK - which was a relief to them all (except for H. Romonov, Manager, Launch Pad Prefabricated Erections, who was masturbating quietly in a corner over the centrefold of Big Buoys magazine and didn't even notice. He was sick of space travel and launch pads. He had decided he wanted to be a sailor).

There was, however, a problem with an exterior video camera, used to check on the skin of the space station – "part of the lens is misted up, or there's something sticking to it," the Colonel reported.

"Well, get out there and check it out," snarled Von Schweinhund.

The colonel – feeling very tender – sent his lieutenant.

Miss Power's head ached, and she was sore all over, but she went. She would do anything for the Colonel. She had fallen head over heels in love with him, interpreting his cold, aloof attitude as playing hard to get. She was sure that love would bloom out of their close relationship. At the very least she would have had a space-child – his child. Anastasia knew that as soon as she could confirm that the space station was operating normally, they could try again. She was ever the optimist.

When she returned, the substance she had scraped off the lens of the exterior video camera was quickly broken down chemically and the ingredients computer-analysed.

"It's cow plop," Buchov told his boss.

"It's what?" Von Schweinhund couldn't believe his ears.

"Yes, you know, cow muck. From cows. Frozen solid because of the cold, but definitely rich cow shit. British breed. Herefordshire heifer I would guess."

Von Schweinhund was purple with rage. A vital experiment ruined. A narrow escape for a space station and its crew, a rebuff for the joint space effort.

"Vot is going on in the world," he screamed. "The Yanks they aim to put men on the moon. We build laboratories in space. The British? They try and shoot us down with cow plop!"

When passions had cooled (much to the disappointment of Anastasia) Von Schweinhund spoke to his Colonel on a private line. "The question is, " he said, "what was it that propelled the cow plop with such velocity into space?"

Buchov had already had the same thought.

"I have further tested the sample and discovered minute evidence of a strange explosive compound, with a peculiar aroma, like green apples. We have nothing like it," he confided.

"Does Miss Power know of this?"

"I think not. Her head is full of romance. She is obsessed with ideas of getting me into the sack."

"Then you must distract her while we investigate what sort of energy force the British have invented. We must keep it to ourselves. It could be a breakthrough in missile propulsion. It might even revolutionise space travel."

"If that is an order, then so be it," sighed the Colonel.

"Your Fuhrer will be grateful," said Von Schweinhund, clicking his heels, quite forgetting himself.

And so Britain, unwittingly, entered the space race, and nearly destroyed the Russian space station to boot. When the Ruskies had recovered from the shock they decided they needed more information on the propellant that could send cow plop so much further than the wind generated by your average Friesian.

When the telephone rang at No 113 Avenue Road, Sandown, Red Harry Hawkins thought it would be Daphne from the pub. He hadn't been in touch with her for a few days, for no other reason than the fact that he had started a relationship with the barmaid at the Flying Pig.

If it is Daphne, he thought, I'll lay on the charm. Nothing wrong with keeping two going.

But it wasn't her.

Moments later Harry left the house with his collar up and went to a public telephone box.

"Lots of sausage," he said when his call was answered.

"On the plate," said someone on the other end.

That was all. But it was enough. It was the signal. Back in the privacy of his home Harry hugged himself with glee. The first phone call had been from a contact at the Russian Embassy. Nothing was said. Harry didn't even pick it up before it rang off. Three rings and the caller put it down. It meant that no-one could trace the call, and yet it was a signal Harry could recognise, after all those years.

The second call was an exchange of code words. It meant, quite simply "Sleeper awake."

CHAPTER 10

YES, you've guessed it. Harry was a Russian agent. He had been approached during a visit to Moscow as a delegate at a trade union conference back in the early 50s. A busty hotel waitress smiled a little too eagerly at him, allowed herself to be coaxed into his bed, and then quickly disappeared while two heavies in long coats and fur hats entered the room, showing Harry compromising photos.

"Bloody hell, that was quick. You have to wait a week for them to print photos at Boots," said Harry.

He wasn't bothered about the photos – for a start there was no-one at home who would worry about what he was getting up to, and secondly he quite liked the idea of working for the Russians. He supported their socialist ideals, they promised him a couple of Black Sea holidays, and yes, they said, they would get the waitress back, so he signed up on the spot.

And now, at last, they had contacted him to indicate his services would be required. It was a surprise, given that his old Commie bosses had been discredited and lost power – he had begun to think he had been forgotten. Why they wanted him now was a mystery. Despite the recent bomb blasts in the town, he doubted a Communist revolution had hit the streets of the Isle of Wight. No, it would be something far less obvious.

He paced his living room, trying to work it out. And then, to get rid of the adrenalin coursing through his veins, he practised petrol bomb throwing – leaping out from behind the sofa, hurling cushions at the cat.

And then he decided to do something positive, in the spirit of the Revolution.

His phone call to the police station caused panic.

Nerves had been on edge all day since the explosion in the field behind Arthur O'Flaherty's pig farm. A thin green mist still hung over the scene and Arthur was trying to calm his pig Polly, who was running around her pen with a strange look in her eyes.

He reported seeing two boys in the vicinity, but police enquiries proved fruitless. There was little damage, so they returned to base not knowing whether it had been another bomb or just a big Chinese firework.

Harry called from a telephone box in the town centre, disguising his voice with a Welsh accent and a handkerchief. It was 2am and Pc Cartwright, who was on night duty, was so excited he switched on the national emergency siren (it dated back to air raids in the war) on the roof, just above the police flat where Supt Blunder was sound asleep, dreaming of policewomen in black stockings.

It's difficult to describe the feeling you get when woken abruptly in the dead of night by a siren designed to alert the deafest member of the community to the danger of a German bomber raid, situated just above your head. Suffice to say that Blunder, still with that smile on his face, left his bed with such velocity that his pyjama bottoms remain undisturbed, cuddled to his hot water bottle. He then hid in the wardrobe.

Having roused the whole town, Pc Cartwright turned the siren off sheepishly, and coaxed his superior back to reality with a hot, sweet cup of tea. All over Sandown people crawled out from beneath their beds and peered out of windows at one another. Some waved.

"It was some Indian chap on the phone, warning us that he had planted a bomb at Cuckoospit Hall," said the constable. It had to be taken seriously, particularly as Cuckoospit Hall was the home of Sir Humphrey and Lady Potts.

They wound back the taped telephone call. "Sounds more like Scottish to me," said Sgt Watson, who had arrived in his slippers.

A motley crew of local officers were gathered together (the anti-terrorist squad had gone back to London for a darts match) and sped to Cuckoospit Hall, where they assembled in the lounge.

A small dog, brown and white with ears that stuck straight up and turned over at the points, thrust itself upon Pc Cartwright's leg.

He tried to shake it off, but it had the persistence of a limpet.

Sir Humphrey wandered in. He looked half asleep. Blunder hardly recognised him, his previously bald head now covered in tight curls. He assumed it was a wig.

"Have you seen anything suspicious?" Blunder asked Sir Humphrey.

"There was one chap..."said the town's most distinguished citizen. He was fresh out of bed with his shirt tucked in his underpants.

"Which chap?"

"Over by the wall, just now. Saw him clearly from my window in the moonlight. Very shifty looking. Did a wee in a rhododendron bush."

"Describe him."

"Had on a silly hat like football fans wear, red and white stripes I think. A blue anorak and slippers."

They all (apart from Pc Cartwright, who was trying to shake Poo Poo, Lady Potts' dog, from his leg whilst pretending it didn't matter anyway) looked at Sgt Watson, who quickly took off his red and white woolly hat, and wished he had gone to the loo before he left the station.

"I'm afraid that was me."

"Oh, was it? Yes, it probably was. Disgusting."

Lady Potts arrived. She was wearing a pale blue dressing gown with a plunging neckline that made them all stand a little bit taller. "I see you've made friends with Poo Poo," she said, grabbing the dog by its collar and pulling him off the young officer, who looked very relieved, "he obviously likes you."

"Poo Poo?" queried Pc Cartwright.

"He's a little shit," said Sir Humphrey.

"Someone broke in once before," Lady Potts continued. "Humphrey was here on his own. They smashed a window but the dog frightened them off. He's very brave."

Blunder was incredibly attracted to her. She sat down on the sofa. He was determined not to look at the curve of her lower leg. He found himself staring at the swell of her bosom, instead.

"Did they steal anything on that occasion?"

"No. but they hit him over the head," said her Ladyship. "Left him bleeding under the window. Been odd ever since, gets spells of aggression."

Blunder looked sideways at Sir Humphrey, who's eyes were drooping. He didn't look very aggressive.

"We will have to search the house and garden. It may have been a malicious false alarm but we can't take any risks," he explained.

So they did. There was nothing.

They returned to the lounge. Sir Humphrey was asleep. Lady Potts was showing even more cleavage and a little more leg. "All clear, your Boobyship, sorry Ladyship," blustered Blunder.

He stepped backwards in embarrassment and trod on the dog, which bit him.

His shout of pain awoke Sir Humphrey, who – dreaming of a cliff rescue – kicked wildly out at a flock of attacking seagulls and knocked Blunder into a hat stand. Poo Poo the dog wasted no time in leaping upon the fallen officer's right leg, thrashing frantically.

"Brain damage," said Lady Potts apologetically, as she pulled him off and helped Blunder up.

"Maybe he should resign from the Police Committee," he grumbled.

"Not my husband, Superintendent! The dog!"

Out on the cliff path, hidden in the shadows of a majestic oak, Red Harry watched the police vehicles arrive and depart. He had no intention of carrying out a bomb attack on Sir Humphrey, or anyone else, unless specifically instructed to do so. He just wanted to shake the old fool up a bit, and spread a little confusion.

It is fair to say that the police were panicking. So much so that when important evidence presented itself to them, in the shape of Sgt Watson's son Bogey and his pal Andrew, they turned it away.

After the incident in the field behind the pig farm, the lads had decided that the best thing to do was destroy all the bottles as safely as possible, without involving the police. But when they went down to the pier to collect those bottles left in the pavilion, they discovered it was roped off because of the damage inflicted in the collision with the Sandown Queen, with a bobby on duty.

And when Andrew went home to get his last remaining bottle, his mum said she had given it and a lot of other rubbish to Miss Beryl Bloggett, the traffic warden, to help raise money for abandoned cats. They understood she would be manning the white elephant stall at a Spring Fete on the recreation ground in several weeks time.

They felt they had no option but to inform the authorities about the danger. So Bogey told his dad about the explosion they had caused, and their concern about the other bottles of Heaven Scent.

"You haven't been sniffing that model aircraft glue again, have you?" said his dad. Nonetheless, he reported the conversation to Supt Blunder, who simply laughed at him. "Don't be daft, they're having you on" he said. "Who ever heard of exploding after-shave? It's not April Fools Day, is it?"

And he left it at that.

"Not our fault any more," said Bogey.

"We've done all we can," agreed Andrew, "apart from getting hold of my uncle's bottle somehow. Maybe we should just wait, and then go to the fete and try and buy that other bottle back before someone else does."

It seemed like a good idea.

CHAPTER 11

CHARLIE had been to Shanklin Hospital to see the young woman they had rescued. "I reckon I'm in there," he said. "She's a darling. I asked her out when she's fit, and she said she would think about it. Jemma also wanted to know if you were going to visit. You should have come."

It was something Tim wanted to put off for the time being.

He had been staying in quite a bit, avoiding Daphne. Of course it was nice to have a girlfriend when it's an uncomplicated relationship but this wasn't the case. The sex was great, and the odd free pint, but the disadvantages were obvious – on one hand she was already married, and on the other Harry Hawkins had a claim on her, and he sounded more and more like a homicidal maniac every time she talked about him.

"Afternoon, Tim," Harry had said only that morning, his usual sarcastic greeting to anyone who arrived for work after he'd started. Tim wondered what Harry's reaction would have been had he been aware that he had spent a considerable time the previous evening (the dog was tied up in the garage) with his wrists and ankles secured to a bed with red ribbon and a big red bow around his person, while Daphne tried to arouse him with nude somersaults and a can of spray cream.

"It is your birthday," she cooed in a quiet moment.

"No it's not..."

"Well, I like to pretend it is."

With that, she sprayed an extra large dollop of cream on a part of his anatomy that took his breath away, and ended the debate.

It MUST have been his birthday!

He liked Daphne, always had, but she was getting a bit too keen. And she didn't get on with Smithy – she had pretended to like him, but gave up the pretence after he let loose the most appalling smell from under the bed at a climatic moment.

"Why do you keep him? He a real stinker," she said. Smithy scowled at her and slunk away to the hall. Tim could hardly explain that if it was a choice between the two he would choose Smithy, any time.

CHARLIE went to the corner café. He fancied an ice cream. A surly girl waitress attended. He quite fancied her.
"What flavours do you have?" he asked.
"We've got lots."
"Well, which ones?"
"What do you want?"
"What about caramel and banana."
"We don't have them"
"OK, chocolate and lemon."
"We don't have them either"
"What do you have?"
"Vanilla, strawberry and raspberry."
"OK, I'll have them."
"We've run out of raspberry and the strawberry has gone orf" she said.
"Vanilla would be lovely. Would you like to come out for a drink with me?" he said.
"Get lost," she said
And the ice cream was rubbish.

ARTHUR O'Flaherty sat at the bar in the Frog and Trumpet. Normally the area around him would empty, all the other customers packing into the far end of the bar. But today nobody moved away, and Arthur enjoyed the feeling. He felt wanted.
"You're Mr O'Flaherty, aren't you?" said Harry, walking over to stand next to him. Daphne, on the other side of the bar, stuck her nose in the air and flounced away. She wanted nothing to do with Harry. Not that Harry was bothered, with much more important matters on his mind, although her husband noticed and thought it very odd.
"Yes," said Arthur, "it is indeed me."
"Only I know your son, Charlie, nice fellow, works at the Chronicle."
"You're that Communist bloke, aren't you?" said Arthur, not known for his discretion.

"Indeed, or so some would say. May I say how very nice that after-shave is that you're wearing."

Arthur smiled with pleasure. His reputation was founded on the aroma that surrounded him. But, as he was only too aware, it was the unpleasantness of the smell that usually caused people to notice him. You can't be a pig man without some of the scent rubbing off on you.

Every morning he drove his lorry around the town picking up the flotsam and jetsamof the previous night's haute cuisine, not forgetting rotten fruit and veg from the greengrocer, bloodied sawdust from Mabel the butcher lady and assorted culinary debris of doubtful origin from the Chinese restaurant on the corner. You could hear him coming a couple of streets away – the rattling of bins, the barking of dogs that followed him in a quarrelling pack, the shrieks of seagulls hovering close each time he slowed.

It was a life he loved.

But he was lonely. And today he intended to do something about it. Which is why he had popped in at Charlie's for a shower and splashed on some of his son's Heaven Scent before nipping in to the pub for a confidence booster.

"Yes indeedee, very nice," continued Harry. "I'd like some myself. Get it from Boots did you?"

"It's Charlie's. I just borrowed it," said the pig man.

"So you don't know where he got it from?"

"Nope. Sorry."

Harry gloomily wandered back to the table where his mate Sid Pugh – who had been let in on the mission – was waiting.

"Any luck?" asked Sid.

"No. It might be the one. But it might not. It certainly has a fierce smell. Makes the eyes water. What I want to know is – how the hell can we tell which perfume they want us to find? There are so many different sorts. Like sniffing out a tart in a massage parlour."

"I'll come with you," said Sid.

"Where to?"

"The massage parlour."

Harry groaned. It wasn't even worth explaining it to him.

"My mum works for him," said Sid.

"What, old Arthur O'Flaherty?"

"Yep. Just started. Cleaning. Says it's in a right state."

Harry sipped his beer and turned the problem over in his head.

His contact man had arrived on a motorcycle, wearing a crash helmet with a red stripe down the middle, just as Harry had been told. They had walked on the beach, skimming pebbles across the surface of the sea, while his instructions were passed.

"You don't need to know why we want to get hold of this chemical formula, suffice to say that it has important potential to our space programme," said the man from the Embassy, who sounded like he had been educated at Eton rather than in a Russian state school.

"And you say it may be disguised as perfume?"

"That's what our scientific experts tell us, old boy. Or perhaps an after-shave. The police were tipped off, but they don't realise the significance of it. The experts say it smells like green apples, although personally I thought it was more like peanut butter and jelly, which I am jolly fond of. With a pot of Earl Grey, of course."

"And it may have something to do with the explosions we've been having in the town?"

"Indeed. You need to be jolly careful. Discreet and jolly careful. And you may need help. Is there anyone you can trust?"

And that was how Sid came on the scene.

He was a bachelor, an ice-cream salesman who lived with his mum. Mrs Pugh was a colourful character, a widow and mother of eight who had always spoiled him, her youngest. Sid was not too bright, and had appalling fashion sense – his mum had wanted a girl and as a child always bought him clothes in pastel shades, mostly pinks.

He was well-known around town.

"He's one of those, isn't he?" said Phil one day as they watched Sid talking to Harry outside the Chronicle office.

"One of those what?"

"You know, a bit left-handed. Ambidextrous. A foot in both camps."

"I'm not sure what you mean" said Tim.

"Not entirely straight. Likes dressing up."

"Not a macho fisherman like you… ?"

"Well, he's not."

"Actually, I find him more likeable than his mate Harry," said Charlie.

Phil looked at Charlie suspiciously.

"What happened to your beard? It suited you. I think a beard suits a man. Very manly."

"Mmm, thanks," said Charlie, doing a twirl. "I had to get rid of it. Shaved it off and stopped using that after-shave. The beard was going green. Very strange stuff."

Sid was very loyal to Harry. He promised to keep his mouth shut, and Harry didn't tell him much anyway.

They were soon hot on the scent. The problem was that you can't just go up to girls, sniffing, and saying how nice they smell, can you? Not when you look like a Sid.

But they did. They had no alternative. How else could they find an explosive, green-coloured, vanilla and peanut-butter-scented after-shave?

They were thrown out of two pubs and the WI gala on the first day. "Bloody pervs" shouted the Area Superintendent as they retreated.

The following day Sid was punched on the nose in the post office, and Harry was asked to leave Boots by a store detective who didn't like the way he was fingering the ladies' toiletries.

They weren't getting anywhere. A new strategy was called for.

Adopting his Welsh accent, and wearing a false moustache and dark glasses – Harry didn't need to, but he had always liked dressing up (it had been one of the qualities that initially attracted Daphne to him, she being heavily into cross-dressing) – he rang the police station from the Victoria Road telephone box.

"It's a reporter on the Chronicle here," he lied. "Just following up a lead on the bombings. Was there ever any suggestion that the explosions might have been caused by some sort of unstable perfume?"

Didn't know they had any Pakistani reporters on the Chronicle, thought Sgt Watson. "What did you say your name was?"

"Jones. Gareth Jones. A colleague of Charlie O'Flaherty."

Funny name for a Pakistani, though the sergeant. However, if he knew Charlie he must be Ok.

"You must be talking about the kids," he said.

"Kids?"

"Yes, young Bogey, my lad, and his pal Andrew. They came in here with some cock and bull story about exploding after–shave. We regard it as a lot of nonsense. Too much TV, that lad"

"That's all right then. No point following that up. Thanks, Willie Bach," said Harry.

"No, I'm Sgt Watson," said Sgt Watson.

It was the breakthrough Harry had been looking for.

CHAPTER 12

ARTHUR, meanwhile had left the pub and made his way down the High Street to Mabel's butcher's shop.

You had most probably already heard of Mabel before you knew she was Tim's aunt. It was in the national papers. At the time she was a celebrity, but things quietened down as they usually do and nobody thinks twice about it any more.

Apart from the Vicar.

Mabel is in her early 60s, a widow for about ten years. She had always helped her husband in the shop and the day after he died she choked back the tears and went back to work. She was small and frail, but she made up for her lack of muscle with enthusiasm.

"Frightens me, the way she flourishes those knives and choppers," said Mrs Ootwhistle, the Vicar's wife, one morning. "You have to keep your eyes on what she's doing. I'm sure I will find one of her fingers when I open the wrapped chops."

"Yes dear," said old Outie, his mind on his sermon. What should his moral message be that week – do not covert someone's else's wife (this would be partly aimed at himself, as a result of a weak moment when Lady Potts bent over to pick up Sir Humphrey's peppermints after the last Sunday service) or give up something you enjoy for Lent (he was tempted to suggest to his wife that they stopped having her mother round).

A wiser clergyman might have adopted the argument, "Listen to what your missus says, she might just be right." For the very next day as Rev Ootwhistle, the Vicar, walked past the butcher's shop, Mabel lost control of a razor-edged knife in her run-up to a particularly defiant piece of steak. There was a flash of light on steel, a desperate shout of "Four!" from Lady Potts – a keen golfer – who had been awaiting the steak's dissection, and the knife hurtled out of the door and across the High Street, pinning the Vicar by the dog collar to the bosom of a half-naked dancer on a pier show billboard.

Mabel apologised profusely. She climbed up on a stool to extract the still-quivering blade from the billboard, allowing the Vicar to collapse on his still-quivering legs into the compassionate arms (and bosom) of Lady Potts. He thought for a moment he was in heaven.

Of course the incident was soon public knowledge.

CLERIC DEREK: HE'S MABEL'S PIN-UP!! proclaimed the headline of a popular tabloid over a picture of the beaming and unrepentant butcher-lady and the embarrassed Vicar, who had reluctantly agreed, in the spirit of forgiveness and for a donation to church funds, to shake hands with Mabel in front of the billboard to which he had been so unceremoniously pinned.

Arthur had known Mabel for years. While others ducked and weaved as they passed – just in case she unleashed another loose knife or chopper – Arthur always stood tall and proud in the doorway, unflinching as sheep ears and bits of gristle flew about him.

Mabel, being of generous spirit, took him in the yard and loaded him with body bits for his pig food.

If she ever noticed the awful pong that surrounded him she never let on.

And Arthur made an effort, cutting down on the drinking, and generally smartening-up.

For him at least, romance gradually blossomed under the dripping ox hearts. Many the time he tried to summon up the courage to ask her out, but under the accusing gaze of strangled chickens his nerve always failed him.

But this time it was different. He arrived all pink and shining in his best suit, and Mabel looked fondly upon him. He had sprinkled Charlie's bottle of Heaven Scent on his vest before he left home. "I like your after-shave Arthur," she said, "it's like lemon and lime."

It made her toes tingle.

Arthur smiled back over a pile of severed pigs trotters. – "Would you like to come for a walk on Saturday?" he said.

Mabel said she would love to.

CHARLIE was in the pub, celebrating with Millie, who was leaving for a new job in London. He had organised the whip-round for her farewell present. Buoyed up by Burt's best bitter, he staggered up to her half-way through the evening and said: "We'll be sorry to see him go."

"Who?"

He thought for a moment. "Whoever it is that's leaving."

"It's me. I'm the one."

"Oh, thanks for coming," he said, and staggered off.

PHIL was going on about Bridlington fishermen again.

"There's this old chap, grey beard, sits there mending nets with his pipe in his mouth," – he gestured with his hands to illustrate the point – "and he's only got one arm, because he jammed it in a winding winch when he was out alone in his boat one day. Steered back on his own! With one arm! Mends his nets and smokes his pipe! Lovely."

His eyes brimmed with tears at the thought of that brave old fisherman.

And then he started his tuneless whistle. Phil was a great fan of light opera, and routinely murdered some fine songs. He really was a most tiresome person. He was particularly annoying now that Millie was gone, presumably because he had lost his audience.

Charlie and Tim tried to ignore him.

"I did national service," he said, trying to attract attention.

"Oh yeah." They were unimpressed.

"Yep, one of the few."

"There were lots who did it," said Tim. "My cousin did it. The bloke next door did it. He was in Palestine. He was killed there. They have a memorial to all those who died in Palestine, and in Korea."

"Pity they don't have one for your lot. Where were you?" asked Charlie.

"Kettering."

"Not a lot of fatalities there."

"No, but it was hard."

They didn't think there would get a replacement for Millie, but there was.

Sir Humphrey came in on the Monday morning, and he brought his nephew Andrew with him.

"He's the new junior reporter. Look after him," he said curtly, and left.

They already knew the lad, and quite liked him, but it was a surprise. "Hope you are going to get proper training. I haven't got the time to teach you. And just because your uncle is the boss doesn't stop him being an idiot," said Charlie.

Andrew explained he was going to college twice a week to do a journalism course. He'd just left school, and had always wanted to be as reporter. – "My mum fixed this for me. My uncle went along with it, but it doesn't mean to say we get on. I think he's a bit of a berk, actually."

They decided to sit him next to Phil.

"He'll show you the ropes. Are you keen on fishing?" said Charlie, all innocence.

"Not really."

"What about travel?"

"Oh yes..."

"Well, Phil knows a thing or to about travel, don't you Phil?" he said as they approached.

Introductions over, Phil got down to business.

"Ever been to Bridlington?" he said.

"Yes, I.... "

"There's this old chap, grey beard, sits...."

They knew Andrew would settle in nicely.

SIR Humphrey was at that very moment crouched over a basin in the bathroom at Cuckoospit Hall, his hair covered in a black foam, which Lady Dorothy was massaging vigorously into his scalp.

"Do you think this will hide it? I can't go round with a head full of green curls. Think of my position... I'll become a laughing stock, and have to resign from my public duties."

"No–one will ever know," his wife assured him. "This black dye will cover it until the green grows out, or until it falls out."

"Falls out? You don't think I'll go bald again, do you?" he whined.

"Who knows, but it won't bother me if it does. I always liked your nice, smooth head, I'm not turned on by black curls. But what I'd really like to know is how this all happened."

"It must be that after-shave of young Andrew's. Very strange stuff. Glad to see the back of it."

If only he knew...

CHAPTER 13

ANDREW soon made himself useful in the office, making tea, fetching sandwiches and doing the calls to the undertakers, to see if anyone interesting had popped off.

One day he said: "Tim, do you think I'm dynamic enough?"

Tim didn't reply. He was typing with one finger. It took a lot of concentration, even after eight years practice. If it was a particularly exciting story and the thought processes flowed, he typed with three fingers. Which was a subbing nightmare because of all the errors. The Chronicle was renowned for its typographival, whoops, typografical, whoops, typing errors. It featured regularly in the columns of Private Eye.

"No–one seems to notice me or listen to what I say," continued Andrew.

Charlie was going to say something reassuring, but was interested to hear Tim's reaction.

There wasn't one. Tim was attempting to spell 'Antagonistic' and it took all his concentration.

Andrew continued speaking – "I sometimes wish I was like you. You always seem to ask the right questions and get answers. And you, too, Charlie. There's something sort of noticeable about you. Particularly in drink."

Charlie put his hand to his mouth and coughed loudly. It was a diversionary tactic, for at precisely the same moment, he farted. Tim and Andrew knew what to expect. They moved quickly out of range.

The lad had been attempting to perfect the same technique since he first became familiar with it a year or two previously, sitting next to Charlie in the stand at a Sandown Rovers match the night after the Chronicle scribe had wolfed down a particularly suspect Lamb Tandoori at the Taj Mahal in Ceylon Street.

Andrew, however, lacked timing, a crucial element. He enjoyed one spectacular failure, during the headmaster's opening prayers at the school speech day. He coughed and farted, but NOT at the same time. As the reverberations faded, and a widening ripples developed amongst the throng of students as they fought to get way from the noxious fumes, he was dragged out the front and reprimanded before the gathering, VIPs and all.

It had been the most chaotic start to a Speech Day for years, with half the fifth form and two-thirds of the younger teachers in uncontrolled hysterics as the massive hole opened up in the assembled ranks. It persisted until the fumes cleared. Andrew had become something of a folk hero.

CHARLIE covered another hoteliers' lunch. It was something he looked forward to, because the wine flowed freely. They sat at a long table and he took a note of the speeches, and consumed huge quantities of claret.

At the end he was one of the last to leave, squeezing his way along between the chairs and the wall. As he approached the end of the table, another chap approached from the other direction. He looked pissed and was scowling in a menacing way, so Charlie thought he would let him go first.

"Go on," he said, with a flourish of a hand. But the flushed guest just stood there, indicating he should be first.

"No, you first," said Charlie, with a sweeping arm movement, not wishing to upset such an obvious thug.

The man mouthed something back and continued to stand there, defiant, insistent that Charlie should be the one to go-ahead.

And so Charlie did, but they both moved at exactly the same time so that they stood there scowling, face to face... and it was only then that Charlie realised he had been confronting himself in a full-length mirror!

Next time, he thought, I'll have to go a bit slower on the Chianti!

SIR Humphrey decided, in the interests of family, to take Andrew under his wing. It's quite probable that he saw the lad as a future editor of the Chronicle, though Andrew was not at all bothered about that. Every morning the newspaper magnate called at Andrew's house in his Jag, and they made tortured small talk all the way in.

They had to walk through an underpass to get to the office. One morning there was a young man there, in a sleeping bag, with a dog, hollow-cheeked and gaunt, dark rings around his eyes. The young man looked even worse.

"Spare any change Guv?" he whispered.

"Not likely, you're trying to con me!" proclaimed Sir Humphrey, with the self-righteousness of his class. "Go and get a job, stop living off everyone else."

The young man didn't even reply, just slumped back and closed his eyes. Andrew was embarrassed.

The same thing happened the following day. The beggar held up a badly scrawled notice asking for help. Dribble was running from the corner of his mouth, and one eye was closed and matted. The dog lay quiet. – "I bet you've got a car and a flat somewhere. You are a public nuisance, Sir!" thundered Sir Humphrey, and strode on.

"Don't you think you are being a bit hard on him? I think he looks really ill," said Andrew.

"Not at all. He's no more homeless than I am. But I must say he's good – by the look of his skin-colour he must use theatrical paint. And the dog's very well trained, making those pitiful whines all the time."

The next day an elderly man dropped a coin in the young man's outstretched hand as they approached. It bounced out and rolled away.

"Come on man, get yourself together," snarled Sir Humphrey. "No good lying around here all day, you've got to get back on your own two feet."

There was no answer. The man stared back at him with dull eyes.

"I think he might be... " Andrew started to say, but his uncle hurried him along.

"Come on, we've better things to do than talk to down-and-outs."

As they started up the steps, two policeman approached. "Was it you that reported the body, Sir?" asked one.

"Body? It's just a tramp, pretending to be ill to get public sympathy."

Sir Humphrey paused while the policemen went down and investigated.

One of them came straight back out. – " He's a dead ringer for a corpse, Sir. I'll have to close the subway. Looks like he died in the night. I think the dog has been dead for a couple of days."

Andrew felt awful. But his uncle was unrepentant.

"I told you he looked ill. Whatever happened to the welfare state? You just can't get any help, these days," he said.

SEVERAL weeks passed without further incident, apart from a rise in local burglaries. Beryl Bloggett's house at Albion Road had been ransacked but it looked the same as normal. As a precaution against her usual clumsiness, Beryl had previously taken several breakable items for her charity stall around to her friend Mabel, the butcher lady, to look after. Mabel noticed the bottle of Heaven Scent. – "Arthur uses this. It's quite nice," she said.

It was no co-incidence that Arthur's farm had also been burgled. But the intruder didn't look in Polly's sty where the old man had stashed his son's Heaven Scent, planning to use it to give the old sow a rub-down for her birthday.

He was like that, Arthur. Very touchy-feely, just like his son Charlie, if ever he had the chance.

Charlie was still failing dismally on the romantic front. He had tried to get a date with a girl he met at the magistrates' court. She was a shoplifter but had nice eyes and was very fashionably dressed – an outfit she had managed to pick up at Ladies Realm on a previous, far more successful, occasion.

She came on to Charlie after her case ended. "I like your tie," she said, fondling it.

"Thanks. I thought they were very hard on you."

He didn't really. She was given probation and a £20 fine. They both knew she would be back nicking the next day.

"I wondered if you wanted to have a drink?" she said, rubbing his chest.

"Now?" He didn't want to seem to keen.

"When is your deadline, you know, for doing my court report?"

"Well, I do it when I go back to the office. We have time for a quickie."

She smiled. "If you didn't write a report, then we could have longer. At my place."

"You mean, forget about it? Don't mention your case?"

"That's the idea. It's so unimportant. Such a little story, and a big favour to me. I would hate it if my mum found out about me by reading it in the Chronicle. She's sick, you know."

Charlie faltered. She was so pretty and so friendly.

But his professionalism pulled him through.

"I won't use it, but not because I like you or because of your mum," he said. "You're right, it is not much of a story, and it would be better if I could do an in-depth feature on you, why you steal, that sort of thing. We could meet up at my place and have a nice dinner, and some wine, and I can do the interview."

"Without naming me?"

Charlie agreed. After all, it would make great copy. And he had high hopes of a romantic follow-through.

They made a date. She insisted on a slight delay so she could "work out what I want to say."

But she never turned up. And her home address was false. And by that time it was too late for Charlie to write a court report.

"You're very naïve. A pretty girl could do anything to you," said Tim.

"Oh, yes, she could," sighed Charlie.

CHAPTER 14

OLD Iron Balls asked Charlie to write a feature about the Yaverland Home for Wayward Girls. Tim wanted to go, having had some experience of the residents, informally, but the Editor didn't trust him with young women. For some reason he had confidence in Charlie.

Charlie was delighted, but nervous. The Home was well-known amongst the local youth.

It was situated on the edge of town behind high hedges. That didn't stop the young women residents from creeping out through the windows at midnight, selecting a waiting car, and disappearing up to the Downs for some hanky-panky.

When their escapades were discovered, the Matron was replaced by a hard-liner, and the hedges by 6ft wire fences.

"That was almost a year ago now – the girls will be desperate for male company," said Tim. "Imagine all those suppressed female hormones bursting for release, a volcano of female passion, and you in the middle of it. You lucky sod!"

Charlie smiled and brushed limp hair out of his eyes. "You reckon I might be lucky?" he ventured.

"Of course you will. I hear the girls get up to all sorts of things in that place, even nude gymnastics, just for a laugh. Imagine that. It'll be great!"

Charlie's imagination went into overdrive.

He waited at the gate and was then admitted by a burly female orderly. He noticed some curtains move in the upstairs windows.

Ushered into the office, he was welcomed politely by Miss Cockerton, the Matron. She was short and stocky and had a large mole on her chin.

"How are you settling in?" asked Charlie, opening his notebook.

"Let's keep me out of this," said Miss Cockerton, "I will just run you through how we work with these sometimes difficult young women, and then you can ask questions."

And so she did. And it was really boring stuff. Mostly about discipline.

"Do they do sport and things like that? Gymnastics perhaps?" said Charlie, his mind a whirl of bouncing breasts and silken inner thighs.

"Of course not, we have no time for that sort of thing. But we make sure they do go to church on Sundays."

After about quarter of an hour of non-stop tedium, a loud alarm suddenly went off.

Miss Cockerton rose and rushed to the door. "Excuse me for a few moments," she said.

Almost as soon as she had gone, the door opened and two young women stood there. One was short and blonde, the other tall and dark.

"Got any money or fags?" said the tall one.

"You can have both of us for a pound," said the short one.

"You speak for yourself. I'm not like that," the dark girl admonished her.

"Oh, uh, no, sorry, I don't smoke and only got a few bob," said Charlie. "Anyway, I wouldn't want to pay for anything."

"Who do you think you are, getting all uppity?" said the short blonde.

"Is that your car, the black MG?" said her companion.

"No, mine's the blue mini-van"

"How many shillings?" said the short one, who was very bargain basement.

"Matron will be back soon," said Charlie nervously.

"No she won't, we let off the fire alarm and then locked her in the dorm."

"You could come and take me out sometime," said the dark-haired girl. "But you can't ring me here."

"Do you like gymnastics?" he asked. "I heard you girls do a lot of it."

"Someone's pulling your plonker" said the blonde.

"What about it, taking me out?" persisted the tall girl.

"You could ring me. I work at the Chronicle. My name's Charlie."

The blonde snorted. "Not sure why you're interested in him. Look at him, he's got limp hair and spots, and no money and a rubbish old van."

"Times are hard," said the dark-haired girl and Charlie together. And they both laughed.

"HOW did it go? Did you score?" said Tim when Charlie returned.

"It was good. I met a nice girl."

"Any gymnastics?" Tim added mischievously. Andrew grinned, sharing the joke.

"Not yet, but you never know."

And that was all he would say.

AFTER much persuasion, Tim had gone to see Jemma who was still in Shanklin Hospital. Her burns were better and she was more than ready to go home.

Tim felt a little easier about seeing her because his turbulent relationship with her sister Daphne had finally foundered on the rock of Smithy's uncompromising hostility. Basically, the dog bit her.

"You shouldn't have tried to get him from under the bed. He felt backed into a corner and reacted," explained Tim.

"I couldn't put up with those awful smells," said Daphne, and she stormed out, nursing a slightly grazed finger, and threatening to report him to the police. But she didn't.

Tim and Jemma clicked at once. Tim knew he was lost the moment he looked into those soft, brown eyes. Her gaze was steady, not challenging, just questioning. He introduced himself, and said how sorry he was not to have visited her before.

"I had been wondering when you would come to see me," she said. "I wanted to thank you for... for... "

Her words tailed off. It was as if, as their eyes met, they each touched the other's soul. Tim was short of breath, and his hands were trembling.

He took her hand – "Anyone would have done it. I'm just glad it was me."

They chatted about his life and her background, but Daphne was never mentioned. Tim wondered if Jemma knew something and had avoided the subject of her sister deliberately. It turned out she loved dogs, and when she was at last able to go home Tim went to see her at her flat the following week. He took Smithy with him. The dog positively purred, if that's possible. He sat with his head on her lap and enjoyed being stroked. Smithy not Tim.

Meanwhile, the police had a series of bomb hoax calls from various telephone boxes, but were getting bored by the whole thing. The anti-terrorist squad started to go home at weekends and Supt Blunder ceased wearing his bullet-proof vest and a Reader's Digest stuffed down his Y-fronts.

You could tell it was the beginning of spring because Greg was constantly being called out to take photos of blackbirds building nests in bicycle wheels and under car bonnets, the local woods were besieged by budding entrepreneurs digging up daffodil and bluebell bulbs to sell on their market stalls, and Arthur was busily picking up his pet rabbit's dried turds from the dining room floor at Saddleback Farm, before he hoovered up.

It was Mabel's idea that he did a spot of spring cleaning. – "It's a terrible mess, dear. You can hardly expect me to want to move in while it's like this," she said.

To tell the truth, Arthur didn't remember the subject coming up, but it wasn't a bad idea.

Their relationship had blossomed. They went for quiet country walks and enjoyed a drink at the pub. Once, Arthur took Mabel out in the cab of his lorry and they parked in a quiet layby.

They snogged. Both feared their dentures might come loose. They breathed heavily, but that may have been general shortage of breath. They wanted heavy petting but their fingers could no longer undo buttons with the speed they needed to maintain the excitement. The cab windows, however, were steamed up, which was something of an achievement.

The next day Mabel visited the farm to help Arthur clean out the sties. She was standing there, knee-deep in muck, a cloud of flies circling her head, when Charlie and Tim called in. "You certainly know how to give a girl a good time," said Tim.

Arthur had been conscious of the fact that the farm needed a woman's hand for some time. That was why he had employed Mrs Pugh as a once-a-week cleaner. But she was a disappointment, restricting her duties to dusting around the lounge and kitchen and then rushing off to do Sid's tea. And Arthur always had to drive her home.

Today she hadn't turned up at all. So Horace the rabbit – denied the freedom of the house – sulked in a hutch next to the pig sties, while Arthur spent a couple of hours up to his elbows in sinks full of washing up and inches of dust. He was determined to be a cleaner, sweeter smelling person, in a tidier, more fragrant house, and to get a respectable job.

By mid-afternoon he had finished with the vacuum cleaner, just in time for his job as a newspaper-seller.

It wasn't exactly a profession, but it was a start. He wanted to better himself. It had taken him three attempts to get on the payroll of the Isle of Wight Guardian, an evening paper with a small circulation at Shanklin. As you know, newspaper sellers are often even more weird than journalists, although usually frequenting the same pubs.

You might think that to get such a job you would need only to be able to shout the unintelligible highlights of the latest edition to the uncomprehending hoards, and to do it in all weathers. You would be wrong. There has to be something about a paper seller to distinguish him from others. They must be NOTICEABLE.

They might, as in the case of one man the Chronicle employed, be an intellectual, which revealed itself by the way in which he not only shouted out every headline, but commented on it – such as "POLICE CLOSE IN ON BOMBER, the useless buggers haven't got a clue" and "MAN JAILED FOR TOWN HALL FRAUD, would you believe he only got a year, that's your money and mine we're talking about."

Or it might be a physical characteristic, like the man who always had the busy spot outside the bus station: Mondays to Wednesdays he wore a dark suit and trilby, Thursdays to Saturdays a green or pink dress with matching eye shadow, stilettos and ear rings. "I like to relax as the weekend approaches," he confided to punters.

At his first interview, Arthur mentioned his disability.

It was not striking enough. But they gave him a second chance.

He got through his second interview by mentioning his missing leg AND inventing mood swings, which so intrigued the interviewer that Arthur was allowed to have a trial, under observation.

He stood outside the post office, alternating between passive indifference and aggressive confrontation, eyeballing potential customers and demanding they buy a paper.

"Do you want one?" he demanded of a passing nun.

"No thank you, my good man," she replied sweetly.

"Well sod off then!" he shouted.

The Head of Circulation (Street), watching from the doorway of the men's lavvy, thought he showed promise, but he asked Arthur to come for a third interview before he made up his mind. The job was, after all, at the cutting edge of newspaper sales.

Arthur turned up in dark glasses, and it got him the job. "Yes, you might just tug at their heart strings," mused the Head of Circulation (Street).

So there Arthur stood, outside the Chronicle office – a popular patch – trying to sell the Guardian, and it wasn't long before Sir Humphrey came out of the office, still in the carpet slippers he liked to wear at his desk (he suffered a little from gout) to remonstrate with him.

"You can't sell that here – it's our rival!" he exclaimed, tearing a copy from Arthur's hand and tossing it into the street.

"Ave pity on a poor old war hero," said Arthur, "blind and incapacitated, and trying to earn an 'onest crust."

"You're no war hero. You're Arthur O'Flatly, father of that layabout Charlie. I recognised you at once by your general scruffiness and by your leg, or rather lack of leg. You probably didn't even go to war, and you certainly aren't blind. Go on, hop it."

"It's O'Flaherty. Not Fart, not Flat, O'Flaherty," said Arthur, annoyed. "Anyway, I don't know him. I lost me sight and me leg in the Battle of Britain."

Sir Humphrey snorted – "Move on I say, before I call the police, with whom, I might point out, I have some clout."

"Lady Dorothy wouldn't like it, treating a poor disabled man like this... "

"How do you know who I am?" exclaimed the newspaper boss, triumphantly, "unless you can see?"

"By your bluster, and general unpleasantness. It's widely known," said Arthur.

Sir Humphrey paused – "Look," he said, at last, "you can stay here until 4'oclock. That's my best offer. What's the time now?"

Arthur fell for it. He peered above his glasses at the Chronicle clock, old grinder as it was known. "It's 3.30," he said.

"Got you!" snarled old Pottsie, grabbing Arthur by the shoulder, unbalancing him. His false leg – which he had bent up against a wall to hide – came down.

"So there's your other leg – it looks perfectly sound to me!" snorted Sir Humphrey in triumph. "You've been having us on for years, haven't you...?"

And in his rage, he kicked it.

A howl of pain echoed up the High Street.

"What happened to him?" asked Charlie, as they carted old Pottsie off to hospital, with a suspected fractured toe.

"He found out that I really did have a metal leg," grinned his dad.

When he got back to the farm, Mrs Pugh was there. She was making herself a cup of tea.

"As you can see, it's all nice and tidy," she said.

"It was like that when I left."

"Well, I polished it up a bit. And I hope you didn't mind me finishing off the caviar."

Arthur was puzzled. "What caviar"?

"You know, on the plate. I never had any before. Nice and crunchy – I can still taste it between my teeth."

And she pointed at the table where Arthur had left a plate full of rabbit poos. The plate was empty.

CHAPTER 15

CHARLIE dropped in at the Phone Inn. It was a bar on the Esplanade. Usually it closed from September until the end of May, but that winter it had stayed open because of the refurbishment.

The idea of the place was quite unusual, certainly along the South coast. Basically you sit down at the bar or a table and there's a telephone in front of you with a large number on it.

A waitress brings you a drink, and there you are, Joe Cool, perusing the talent at the other tables, and trying to work up the courage to dial the number of anyone you fancy.

It would have been a lot easier if Charlie's uncle's mobile phone idea had worked!

Charlie hadn't been in there for a few weeks, He sat there for a few minutes looking at the talent. No-one rang his number. He sat looking glumly at the sea. Far out a ship's lights were bobbing up and down as it negotiated a heavy swell away from the sheltered coastal waters. He wished he was on it. He gulped his beer and thought about leaving.

When the phone rang it made him jump. He picked it up quickly because people were looking.

"Can I join you?" said a husky voice.

"I suppose so... who are you?" – he looked wildly around. Most people were just sitting, although one or two were engaged in animated telephone conversation. Charlie saw a blonde at the bar, smiling at him.

"Yes, I guess you see me," she said, in a soft American drawl. "Do I pass inspection?"

"Of course.... come on over."

It was turning out to be quite a night.

The girl joined him and he bought her another drink. She said she was from Oregon and was over in the UK to work for a few weeks. She was very pretty and her glasses actually suited her. Charlie was a bit slow with the conversation, not being used to chatting up girls. They sat in silence looking out across the bay.

He asked her where she was working.

"It's a newspaper here, starting next week. I'm a journalist, working through an International Fellowship."

"Not on the Chronicle?"

"Sure is... why?"

Charlie explained. She laughed, and said how nice it was to meet him, and they shook hands. Her name was Annie. He knew that Tim would be thrilled. But he needed to get in there first.

"Are you keen on gymnastics" he asked hopefully.

"I've done quite a bit. Why?"

"Oh, nothing, it just interests me"

And then she said she had to go.

"I have a few matters to see to," she said.

He watched her bum moving as she walked to the door. It made him feel good. She turned and waved and it made him feel even better.

It was strange that old Iron Balls hadn't mentioned her, but that's the way he operated. Kept everyone in the dark. The less they knew, the less chance they had of objecting to it. But this time there would be no resistance. She was, as they say, a honey.

THE editor popped in for a few moments to introduce Annie on the Monday morning, and then went off to the golf club.

"He's not exactly a 'hands on' Editor," Tim explained.

"I could be a 'hands on' reporter," said Charlie hopefully, but Annie let the moment pass.

It worked very well. The girl had confidence and wrote sharp copy and was pushy enough to get a story. It was a pleasure to show her around town. Andrew seemed to dote on her, asking loads of questions about life in the US. Eventually they agreed that she would do police calls every other day, and the odd women's page story when it arose, although she made it clear she was not into that sort of soft journalism.

She was particularly interested in the bombings, reading through all the cuttings, and interviewing Supt Blunder about the latest position... which basically was no further advanced than when the first explosion had destroyed Sgt Watson's car.

"They don't seem to have a clue, and even the green liquid they found on the police van was too small to be analysed properly, although there was a hint of phosphorus," she said.

She sat Andrew down and questioned him closely about that incident. The lad was visibly reluctant to say much about it, which she took to mean he was embarrassed by the fact he had been on the beach with a girl at midnight.

"I think it was the after–shave, but the police say it wasn't. They laughed at me," he said.

"That's very interesting. Have you any of it left?"

The lad said he hadn't, and she seemed disappointed.

"What happened to it?"

"Well… one was in the police car that blew up, another we used to destroy a cow pat, a third went to my uncle old Pottsie which my aunt gave away for a charity bottle stall. The fourth one mum gave to Captain Smith, and that must have been destroyed when the boat exploded."

"And then there was a fifth bottle that you had on the beach with Angela Braithwaite," interrupted Tim. "What happened to that?"

"It was in the police van that exploded."

"Then there were the bottles that I gave to Charlie," said Andrew.

They all looked at him.

"I haven't used much of it," he said. "Old Arthur seems to have taken one of them over. Trying to get rid of some of the pig pong."

"So there are three left, Charlie has one, one is destined for some charity stall and the third is with Charlie's dad," summed up Annie.

Andrew didn't tell her about the bottles left on the pier. He thought she was a bit too interested. He decided to talk to Tim about it later.

"The whole thing stinks," said Phil.

"What do you mean?" asked Annie.

"The way they are crippling the British fishing industry, by reducing the catch quotas. There won't be any boats left out of Bembridge soon."

"What's that got to do with the bombings?"

"Nothing. I was just pointing it out. And don't use the office phone for your calls. It's compromised. Use a phone box."

And he went back to subbing the sports page.

Annie looked at Tim and raised her eyebrows.

Red Harry came in to the newsroom. He was being remarkably friendly to Andrew, considering he was Sir Humphrey's nephew.

"Anything I can do to help, let me know," he said. "I'd be only too pleased to show you the machine room and explain how it all works."

"Thanks, that would be great."

Tim found Harry's presence unnerving, but the union man didn't seem to notice.

He stood behind the lad, who was one-finger typing a death report.

"That's a nice after-shave you have on, my lad," he said.

Andrew was puzzled – "After–shave? Not me. Must be someone else."

"Must be your natural fragrance," said Charlie.

Annie, who had been on the phone, walked over and shook Harry's hand – "I've heard all about you, Mr Hawkins," she said, which surprised Tim because he was not their usual topic of conversation. "You are a key man here, I guess."

"Without my finger on the button, the presses would not roll," he said pompously.

She held on to his hand just a little too long. She was not usually that friendly.

Tim wondered why.

"Perhaps you could give me the tour at the same time as Andrew?" she asked.

Harry was delighted.

ANDREW waited for the No 47 bus to work. It was late. He had eaten a dodgy kebab the night before and was now suffering terrible wind. There was no-one about so he decided to relieve the pressure. Unfortunately, as he negotiated the delicate balance between breaking wind and accidental follow-through, it delayed the moment long enough for the bus to turn sharply round the corner just as he released the gas.

He was followed onto the bus first by the noxious fumes and then by the Vicar, who had made a mad dash to the bus stop on his way to the Young Mother's meeting, having been delayed by coffee and buns with the WI.

Andrew stumbled to the nearest vacant seat overcome with guilt as the appalling pong gradually spread its dreadful fingers into every corner of the bus. "Cor mate, that's a pong-and-a-half," whispered the chap next to him, edging away. "I'm surprised the conductor didn't make you buy an extra ticket for that one."

It was unfortunate for Rev Ootwhistle that, not only did he also become a victim of the foul fumes but was mistakenly identified as the perpetrator, for as the bewhiskered gent next to Andrew finished talking to him, an elderly woman behind leant forward and said loudly: "Don't blame him, it was the Vicar that done it. There was no smell until he got on. I can see the guilt written all over him."

And, indeed, the Vicar looked shamefaced as he passed down the central aisle. Three passengers, upon smelling the smell and hearing the woman's words, moved over, blocking empty seats to prevent him joining them. Several windows were opened, loudly.

"It's an evil presence, that's what it is," said the woman, who had previously spoken. "Something ungodly has followed him on."

"Don't be absurd" said a woman at the back in a big hat. "He's just got an odour problem, that's all. Nothing more sinister than that. Isn't that right, Vicar?"

"I'm sure it was not me. It was just suddenly there, amongst us," said the Vicar, not wishing to apportion blame.

"It makes me go all hot and cold, it's something creepy, like that ectoplasm stuff," said his chief persecutor.

"I'm going to tell his wife," whispered the woman in the big hat.

CHARLIE had been busy preparing for the next flying machine race.

"You're not going to make fools of us again, are you?" said Tim.

"Course not. This one is a lot lighter and easier to get off the ground."

"What's the idea of the race?" asked Annie.

They were in the newsroom, on a Monday. Monday's were usually a bit quiet. Charlie had been down to cover court, which was unusual, and an usher had mistaken him for a defendant and tried to stop him entering the press area. It was the intervention of Sir Humphrey, presiding, that enabled him to take his seat.

"I must thank you, m'lord," Charlie said.

"That's quite all right, and I'm not a lord, as you well know. Just a Knight of the realm. The use of the word Sir will suffice."

"Then I must thank you again, Sir Knight, for it is after all the freedom of the press that... "

"Please sit down, Mr O'Flaherty," said Sir Humphrey, irritably.

Charlie sat down, but continued to express his gratitude.

"Shall I call an usher to evict him, Sir?" said the clerk to the court.

But Charlie got the message. He was quiet as a mouse after that. Except when he was heard to mutter "I should bloody well think so" as the chairman announced a six month sentence on a man who had not only burgled a local pub, but smashed up all the spirit bottles he couldn't carry, and let the beer run out of the taps behind the bar. To Charlie, a pub was a church, and such vandalism sacrilege.

"Would the press please refrain from commenting on the decisions of the court," declared Sir Humphrey from the bench.

Charlie looked at his fellow hacks, eyebrows raised, a picture of innocence.

After Charlie had finished writing up his court copy, he and Annie went up to the farm to have a look at his handiwork.

The machine was quite bulky, with big aluminium wings and a huge gear wheel. – "We will just give it a shove, pedal like mad and it will soar away," Charlie observed.

"It looks quite comfortable, too," said Annie.

"It should be, it's a double saddle, full of horse hair and chicken feathers from the farm," Charlie explained, adding hopefully "Want to sit on it with me?"

"I'll take your word for it."

When they got back, Harry was in the car park. Tim joined them.

"A little bird tells me you are about to take to the air again," he said. "Or is young Tim going to do another belly flop, like last year?"

"We've just been to see Charlie's flying machine," explained Annie. "It's very impressive, with a wing-fuselage weight and span ratio that should give considerable uplift."

"You actually sound like you know what you are talking about," Tim said, impressed.

"I should, I've had had NASA space engineering training. That was before I got bored with it all and went into journalism."

"So you reckon it stands a good chance?" said Harry.

Charlie laughed – "It's a cert to win."

They planned to have a test flight from a hill overlooking the farm the following weekend, but on the Friday the Regatta committee rang Charlie at home.

"It's off, they've banned me," he later announced in the Frog. "Somehow they found out about the gear system, and they say it gives us an unfair advantage."

"But surely that's what the competition is all about, isn't it?" said Annie. "I thought the idea was to use skill and initiative to develop and fly your own flying machine. That's what you have done, and the gears are just one part of it."

"I argued, but they won't have it. They said a pedal and chain is OK, but no gears. I actually think they've done a deal with the Murphy's pub lot – they have accepted a ban on their hang glider, in return for a promise that they would also ban my gears, so we are both back to square one."

"The question is... how did they find out?"

Tim thought he had the answer - "You know we haven't been seeing much of Harry in the pub lately, well, Daphne tells me she thinks he has been sniffing around the barmaid at Murphys. So that could explain everything."

"The shit!" said Annie with feeling.

It was a whole new side to her character.

CHAPTER 16

IT was Good Friday. The whole town looked forward to Easter because it meant the long, dark evenings were gone, and the visitors about to arrive. The pier had been partially repaired and everyone was looking forward to the re-opening of the pier pavilion, and, the start of the summer variety show, Sandown Follies.

But the event that had really caught everyone's imagination was the arrival of the First Train to Sandown.

"What's that?" enquired their American colleague.

"It's a long story, about six years long," Tim explained. "There was a bloke called Beaching who decided that the best way to improve communication in Britain was to close down all the small railway lines and stations, and make people go by road. Personally, I often wondered if he had shares in Wimpy."

"They build highways?"

"I expect so... anyway, Dr Beaching closed our little railway line to Newport because it didn't do much business in winter. Yes, it carried thousands of holidaymakers here every week in the summer but that was forgotten. I wasn't around in those days. My mum used to tell me about the steam trains and how she loved travelling on them when she was young."

And he told her how the local people fought a long campaign to save the train, but were defeated and the line was pulled up and turned into a footpath. The station became old Ernest O'Flaherty's house and workshop.

Ever since then visitors from Newport had arrived by car and coach, by-passes had been built and car parks provided. "And in case people don't park where they should the town employs a traffic warden, a little woman named Beryl Bloggett, to police the streets and hand out tickets."

"I think I saw her yesterday, in the High Street. There was a crowd round her – someone said she had been knocked down trying to serve a ticket on an ambulance."

"Yep, that's Beryl. She's a bit accident prone."

Tomorrow, Tim continued, would be a great day for Sandown because a millionaire entrepreneur who had bought the Isle of Wight railway line from the government, had – in a display of rare public spiritness and unusual foresight – decided that trains did have a future linking small communities to the great outside world, and was re-opening the railway link to Newport. Even the old station was undergoing a facelift.

"Bravo," shouted Annie, clapping her hands.

"Indeed," said he.

Phil sat smoking and coughing. He usually did both together.

"There are no doctor's appointments over Easter. It's a disgrace," he said.

"Are you ill?" asked Annie.

"I've got a cough, and a bad chest, but they wouldn't make an appointment for me until next week... me with my history of diabetes, sciatica and angina. And then the place will be full of malingerers. The health service is dreadful. I've complained but it makes no difference."

"You should cut out the smoking," said Tim.

"Don't tell me to stop smoking, it's my only pleasure. And it's my right to smoke if I want. I fought for that freedom."

"Sounds to me like you have done quite well out of the health service, getting treatment for all those ailments. I wish we had it in America, " observed Annie.

Phil had a coughing spasm, after which he spat into his waste bin.

"It's all this newspaper fibre in the air that makes me cough. Not the fags. They are the only way to clear-out my chest," he said. "I'm thinking of suing the company for ruining my health."

And then he lit up another.

CHARLIE had received a phone call and made a date with the girl from the Home for Wayward Girls, whose name was Lorna. "I'll pick you up at 4pm and we can go to the pictures or a pub," he said.

"Ok, but I will have to be back by 7.30pm or they lock the doors and treat you as an absconder," she said.

He was excited. It was his first date for... well, years.

Unfortunately, his mini-van wouldn't start.

"Can't you get a bus, or walk?" said Arthur.

"Of course not. I'm trying to impress her. And we can't go far if I arrive on foot or by bus. It's two miles out of town and it's raining."

"Well, what other option do you have?"

Charlie turned up outside the home at 4pm driving his dad's pig lorry. Lorna was waiting by the gate and didn't realise it was him. He could see the curtains twitching in the rooms behind her.

"It's me, get in," he shouted, leaning over to open the door.

"Where's your van? This is an old lorry. And it stinks. I'm not going in that, what would everybody think?"

"The van's broken down. It's the best I can do at short notice."

"Well, I'll not bother. I'm not that desperate. I'll pretend you were a pig man asking directions. Go on, sod off."

So Charlie did. So ended another romantic dream.

ELSEWHERE, however, love blossomed.

Arthur and Mabel went for a walk. They decided to wander across the fields and down by the railway line, to see the train go by. Arthur had splashed Heaven Scent across his chest and, in case he perspired (he was becoming seriously paranoid about unpleasant body odours) took the bottle with him in a coat pocket.

Polly watched him go, and as she caught a whiff of the perfume her snout quivered and a thin stream of saliva dripped from the corner on her mouth. She loved that smell.

The great sow lumbered towards the gate of her pen and pushed hard at it with the side of her head. The gate swung in and the latch fell. In seconds, the gate was open and Polly set off in a brisk if ungainly gait in the direction of the railway line.

At Sandown station, crowds were gathering. It was such a big occasion that the whole of the Chronicle editorial staff were on duty. Annie and Andrew were to interview the arrivals, mostly old folk, while Charlie – still refusing to tell his mates how his big date had gone the previous day – and Tim would do the VIP train trip, returning to Newport and picking up another load of passengers for Sandown.

The station forecourt was crowded. Sir Humphrey was there, and Lady Potts (she had on a pink hat with a huge brim). Harry Hawkins and Sid Pugh stood together, whispering. "You go on the train and watch Charlie in case he has his bottle with him, and I'll stay here and keep an eye on the traffic warden. She must have her bottle hidden somewhere," ordered Harry.

Beryl Bloggett was busy writing down tickets for several cars parked on yellow lines across from the station. They all knew who had left them there. The Anti-Terrorist squad had arrived in a rush, delayed because there latest undercover outfit had been late arriving from Scotland Yard. They stood at the end of platform in a line, trying to look inconspicuous – seven Bobbies in identical police-issue British Rail station staff uniform. Their intention was to identify suspicious passengers and search them.

The train arrived in a cloud of choking black smoke. Rail supremo Dick Pickle thought it a good idea to use a steam loco for the first train, with the result that Sandown fire service had been called out to extinguish five grass fires on the embankment within three miles of the town centre.

The carriage doors opened, and out rushed a hobbling hoard of little old ladies in heavy winter coats and scarves. They had fed generously on Pickle Rail steak and kidney pies, with mash and onions, and Mrs Pickle apple pies.

Mr Pickle waited for them. It had been his idea to hand out special packets of commemorative indigestion tablets to the first 100 people to arrive after using the new service.

He had underestimated the affect of the onions. The ladies advanced upon him in traditional elbows-at-the-ready jumble sale battle formation. He vanished in a scrum of thrusting umbrellas and straining elastic stockings as they headed for the toilets. And then they were gone, dashing down the platform towards the thin blue line of railway staff at the ticket barrier, leaving Supt Blunder to pick up Mr Pickle and wipe crushed wind tablet off his beard.

The Anti-Terrorist squad has seen nothing like it. In years to come when stories of their valour were recalled the siege of

Sandown would come first, far ahead of Ulster and Canary Wharf. They tried to stand solid before the onslaught, but were hemmed in on all sides by jabbering old fogies. Luggage flew as thick as insults. They all looked alike, old and grey and vicious. Any of them could have been a terrorist. Not one person was searched. The bomb squad knew when it was outgunned and out manoeuvred.

Annie, who had managed to intercept an elderly man as he left his carriage to ask him what he thought of the new rail link (it all got very confused because he had his hearing aid turned off and thought she was his long-lost niece Andrea) found herself in the thick of the action.

"Porter, find me a taxi," screamed a busty matron in a tweed suit, thrusting three travel bags into the arms of one startled officer. "No, I was here first – take me to the George Hotel," bellowed a harridan with a face like a pickled sandwich, tearing the bags out of his arms and replacing them with a battered brown suitcase tied up with string.

"Where's the loo?" shouted several frantic voices. "I've lost my handbag," bellowed a burly blonde in a blue dress and suspicious stubble. "I've lost my husband," cried a poor thing in thick glasses and a lop-sided hat with a flower.

Fights broke out in all directions as they competed for the station staff's attention. Suitcases flew through the air and burst on the ground, spilling out voluminous bloomers and emergency toilet rolls. Beryl Bloggett was giving first aid to a young officer who had a metal coat hanger wrapped around his neck when she was hit over the head by a walking stick, and had her thick crepe stockings ripped from her ankles. Only Annie's swift intervention prevented a sweet little old rosy-cheeked lady from nicking the traffic warden's hat.

Two of the policemen had to go to the cottage hospital for treatment, and the other five were last seen loaded-down with suitcases, under the escort of several hard faced grans, heading for bed and breakfast hotels on the esplanade.

Beryl Bloggett? Suffering from concussion and muttering incoherently, she was received at the hospital by the Matron, and placed in her favourite bed under the window, with fine views across the bay.

"She's become very special to us. A bit like a mascot," the Matron confided to one of the officers, who had expressed interest in the fact that she was getting preferential treatment.

Back at the station order had been restored following the departure of the old folk, clutching their stomachs and colostomy bags.

Mr Pickle had got his wind back, too, and sportingly agreed to carry on with the programme. There was free food and drink for townspeople.

Tim's attention was distracted by the fact that Daphne was bearing down on him, breasts thrusting provocatively through a jumper that was a little too thin and much too tight for such a solemn occasion as this.

"How are you, dear Tim?" she said, as if they had never fallen out.

"You're looking very, uh, healthy," he said, for indeed she was. Very fit.

"Yes, I feel very perky. My sister has been here... did you know? Oh, of course you do. Cheered me up lots. It's exciting isn't it, seeing the train. I've just come down for the champers and nibbles."

Tim pretended to be disinterested.

"I had better be going. I have to go on the train to Newport. There's lots of drink and nipples, sorry nibbles, on there, too."

"Ooh, isn't it fun," she squealed in a girlish way that made the hair on his stomach straighten. "I'm coming on the train, too, and so is Jemma. She'll be ever so pleased to see you."

Tim made further excuses and left. How was he going to avoid meeting them together? He went looking for Charlie; maybe he had the answer.

Meanwhile, Andrew had joined Sir Humphrey in a carriage. "He insists I go with him to Newport. I can't get out of it," he told Tim, through the window.

"But you're supposed to be doing interviews here... "

"I had a word with Charlie and he said he would stay."

Sir Humphrey was leaning forward blowing kisses at Lady Dorothy. She had declined to visit his old army friends in Newport.

After all, she was expecting an afternoon call from the Vicar. She DID like the Vicar.

The train whistled twice and left in a cloud of smoke. Sid Pugh stood disconsolately by a window. He had realised Charlie wasn't on the train, having spotted him on the platform trying to chat up a pretty policewoman.

Sir Humphrey and Andrew sat in silence, watching fields speed by. Occasionally the smoke thickened and they passed cursing fireman, hoses whiplashing across the sky as they leapt to avoid fresh cascades of sparks from the locomotive's furnace.

"Oh, happy days," murmured Sir Humphrey, in reflective mood.

Andrew changed the subject – "You're not expecting me to stay overnight in Newport, are you?"

"Of course not," his uncle said grumpily. "It's my reunion. I just thought that it would be nice for us to get together for your mother's sake. To get to know one another."

There was a long, awkward silence.

Just then the train shuddered to an abrupt halt, causing their baggage to leap off the rack.

"There's a great big fat pig on the line," shouted Andrew, peering out of his window.

Everyone crowded to his side, Sid Pugh among them.

CHAPTER 17

ARTHUR and his friend Mabel were enjoying their romantic walk along the embankment when they realised Polly was galloping along the railway line after them, closely followed by the train.

"It's that darn after-shave. I've been giving her a rub down in it, and she loves the smell. She's been following us," groaned Arthur.

"The train will hit her – oh the poor thing," wailed Mabel, who had a deep affection for living, breathing animals, in spite of her enthusiastic approach to them when dead on a slab.

Arthur had an inspired moment. He took out the bottle of Heaven Scent and removed the lid. A sickly, sweet aroma filled the air, and as he waved the bottle around, Polly caught a whiff and stopped abruptly, the fat on her flanks rippling into her neck like a squeezed concertina, before lumbering off the track and heading towards them.

The train ground to a halt, with a massive blast of escaping steam and a squeal of metal grinding on metal.

"I'll try and get her to follow me," shouted Arthur, turning away towards the fields.

But before he had taken a few steps there was a blur of blue and pink, the bottle was snatched from his grasp and Sid Pugh – who had leapt out of the carriage as soon as he saw Arthur waving it around – was dashing back towards the railway line, laughing triumphantly.

"Stop him!" bellowed Arthur.

And Polly did just that. It's surprising how quickly a pig can move, all 20 stone of her, if the occasion arises. It may be because a baked bean and cheese sandwich is on offer (Polly's favourite), or when a suckling infant gives a teat a particularly sharp bite with a new tooth, or perhaps the presence of a barking dog (Polly had long ago established her superiority over Tim's newshound Smithy by backing him into a corner and then squashing him against the wall).

Polly smelt the full strength of the perfume, associated that with the colourful figure looming above her on the embankment, and knocked it over with a toss of her pretty head. Sid rose into the air, a jumble of flailing arms and a whirling rainbow of legs, and the bottle flew sideways into the side of the train...

There was a flash of green....

NOW you may be wondering what happened to that bugger Tim while all this was going on. To tell you the truth, absolutely nothing. He was sitting in the toilet at the back, ignoring pleas for compassion from elderly and young alike who had partaken of Mr Pickle's pies, determined to avoid a confrontation with Daphne and Jemma.

He watched as they climbed on the train. They slipped into the buffet car, sipping free wine and giggling like schoolgirls, while a waiter (or rather train hostess as Mr Pickle would have it) hovered over them.

When the train stopped Tim peeped out of the window but couldn't see anything. He settled back on the seat resigned to the fact that he would be there until they reached Newport. Interviews would have to wait until the sisters were out of the way.

Vaguely he could hear a voice he recognised as Sir Humphrey's shouting, funnelled down the train by the corridor, as they started moving again, and he was just settling back into his reverie when a massive explosion blew the side of the compartment in and hurled him out into the passage with the seat around his neck, his face covered in blood.

He was just about conscious. He could hear the voices of rescuers picking their way through the wreckage, and felt arms lift him down the embankment. He opened his eyes just once – Jemma was holding one of his hands, and Daphne the other. They weren't looking at him, but at each other, and Jemma was saying: "You mean he's the one you have been seeing?"

He was drifting, drifting... perhaps it was all a dream? More like a nightmare.

Back on the track, recriminations flew thick and fast. "Who did that? They ruined my lovely train," complained Mr Pickle.

"It was an exploding pig. I saw it on the line," said the train driver.

Arthur snorted indignantly. "Don't be daft. The pig's here. It was an exploding bottle of after-shave."

"After-shave? Pull the other one," said Mr Pickle. "It must have been a bomb."

"There must have been two pigs, one of which was a kamikaze pig," said the train driver, undaunted.

The bomb squad arrived. They found Sid Pugh bleeding by the side of the line, ragged and torn. They took him into custody.

"My lovely trousers, ruined," sobbed Sid.

"Is that your pig?" shouted the train driver to Arthur, who was still trying to manoeuvre Polly out of the way.

"Indeed it is, and thank you for stopping."

"Nearly caused a h'accident, and there's a bye-law against pigs on the track. It should be arrested."

Mabel tried to coax the big sow off the rail with a pork sandwich, from the picnic she had packed. It was a bit insensitive and Polly stuck her nose up at it. However, with the smell of the after-shave gone, replaced by that of burnt wood and singed flesh from the wrecked train, there was no reason to hang around. She made her own way back to the farm.

They put Sid in the hospital bed next to Tim, with a police guard. Sid was badly concussed and what little hair he had was burned off, but he had escaped the flying glass that injured several others. Superintendent Blunder came in every couple of hours to see if he was fit enough to be interviewed.

"We have reason to believe he is the bomber," he confided to the hospital matron in a loud whisper. "Just a question of tidying up all the evidence, and then there'll be an arrest."

Sid was saying nothing. They had taken away his clothes, but left the shoes. The only time he stirred was when his mother came in, wearing a pair of pink leggings and a yellow blouse with a frill around the neck, demanding that he be allowed home. – "Don't be so silly," she laughed when the policeman on guard told her Sid was likely to be charged, "they don't make you pay when you've been in an accident. This is a national health hospital."

Sid groaned, and turned away.

Miss Bloggett was recovering from her railway station riot injuries in an adjacent ward. She saw Tim, and waved. He smiled back. He didn't want to be near her for any length of time in case anything bad happened. He fell fast asleep.

Pc Cartwright, who was supposed to be guarding Sid Pugh, had a long chat with Beryl Bloggett, who he found quite interesting. She, in turn, was charmed by the young constable. After about an hour, he went back to sit next to Sid's bed, and he too promptly fell asleep.

When Tim woke the constable in the morning, and pointed out that Sid's bed was empty, they hoped that he had simply gone to the bathroom. They were wrong.

"Where's my uniform – someone's taken my clothes. And my cap!" shrieked Beryl Bloggett, standing in front of an empty locker in her nightdress. It had yellow lines down it.

Someone said 'yes, they had noticed a traffic warden' leaving the hospital a couple of hours earlier, and 'yes, the woman did seem to be wearing her hat at a particularly jaunty angle, and with a little too much lipstick on, but she had a nice smile'.

Supt Blunder was inconsolable. They searched Sid's home, watched the bus station and warned taxi drivers, but there was no sign of him. Pc Cartwright was told to stay out all day with his dog until Sid was found. Eventually, he lay down and refused to walk any more. The dog, not the constable.

As for the railway, the track was so badly damaged that the service was suspended until further notice. Dick Pickle had to charter buses to take all the old folk back to their home when their holiday was over. He was unhappy, and so were they. But to his credit, he made an effort, arranging a photo call with the local press to show what a caring businessman he was.

"Rotten old buses with no toilets and no pies," snorted an old girl, sticking the end of her umbrella up his nostril when he met them as they disembarked in Newport.

HARRY sought consolation for the injuries to Sid and the loss of the bottle of Heaven Scent in the arms of the barmaid at Murphy's tavern. He got more than he anticipated. Afterwards, half-way down the stairs, his left knee gave way and he tumbled to the bottom.

He sat there for a moment wondering which bit hurt most, the deep scratches down his back, his knee or the throbbing bruise under his left eye where Mad Maggie Flynn had whacked him with a Jersey Cow hot water bottle at her moment of supreme fulfilment.

He was also suffering from a sprained left shoulder, caused by the same contortion as his knee injury.

"Come back to bed, Harry," cooed Maggie, ready to leap on him from the top of the wardrobe.

Not likely, he thought. He was knackered. No doubt she had devised some new and challenging perversion, ram-rodding him with a vibrator or hot-wiring his testicles. She was insatiable. He had had enough.

He stayed quiet until she thought he was gone. He could hear her snoring. Then he made another call to the police station from the public bar, just to spread a little more confusion.

"It was that Pakistani again. He said he's left a bomb at the Town Hall. I think he's trying to trick us, shall we ignore him?" asked Pc Cartwright.

"No, we had better check it out. There's a big council meeting tonight," said Sgt Watson.

"I'll do a check, just in case we can find out where he called from," said the constable. And he did. And lo and behold, the call came from Murphy's Tavern.

By the time he got there Harry was long gone.

"We don't 'ave any Pakistani gentlemen 'ere," said Maggie, clutching a bathrobe to her.

"Any strange men here last night who could have made the call?" enquired the young constable, nervously. He was unsettled by the way the barmaid kept looking at his groin. He feared his zip was undone.

"Not with my luck," said Maggie, deliberately brushing against his nether regions as she bent to pick up a beer mat. "What I need is a nice young h'officer like you to keep me company."

But when she stood up, he'd gone.

CHAPTER 18

AND so Sandown Council entered the drama. The Mayor had decided to hold a public meeting to discuss the explosions, which had not only terrified local people but had severely hit the number of summer holiday bookings received by local hotels and guest houses. After all, who wanted to go to Sandown to get blown up? Much better to put up with rain in Blackpool.

Charlie, having consumed enough beer to sink the Sandown Queen, was supposed to help Tim report on the meeting at Sandown Town Hall. As he staggered out of the Frog and Trumpet he collided heavily with the Travellers Rest, so he decided to rest for a while in there, too.

He was looking particularly wretched, his green baggy trousers completely at odds with a yellow shirt decorated with parrots. His face was red from the beer and his hair looked like it had been whipped into hysteria with an electric cattle prod.

He made a great attempt to walk straight and appear unruffled as he approached the council chamber. The mayoral procession had already begun, with the Mayor in full regalia marching in behind the town clerk, who was carrying the official seal and mace, and then the councillors. Charlie attached himself to the rear.

As the crocodile of VIPs wound its way through the public seats, a disturbance broke out between Charlie and the Director of Piers, Parks and Public Places – mistakenly referred to in the Chronicle as the Director of Pubic Places – who objected to his heels being trodden on and the smell of alcohol.

"Who is that man. He looks like he's been shipwrecked?" the Mayor hissed.

"He's the Director of Pubic... "said the clerk.

"No, not him, the other one... "

"Oh, he's just a reporter. Charlie something. He seems to be a little late."

"Well, help him find his place."

The clerk glided over to Charlie, who had the Director of Parks, Piers and Pubic Places in an arm lock, and was propelling him towards the door, obviously intent on settling their differences.

"You are over there, in the press seats," said the clerk, gently pulling his arm.

Tim waved at Charlie, and he grudgingly released a very relieved official, and they both sat down.

There was a burst of applause from an unruly section of the audience. Charlie held up one hand in appreciation.

As was customary, Rev Ootwhistle, Council Chaplain, stood up to give a blessing. Following the altercation on the bus, his wife (who had been informed of the problem by a 'helpful' friend) always made sure he had been to the toilet and had deodorant under each arm. He also had on a dash of after-shave and his wife's pink bloomers, but she didn't know about that.

The company rose with their Chaplain. But just as he started to pray, Charlie dropped his pen. It rolled across the floor and under a row of councillors' chairs.

"Leave it," Tim said quickly.

But he wouldn't. He was not in the mood to listen. He looked at the pen, and then at Tim, and back at the pen. He was as restless as a wasp caught in a tight-rope walker's tights. And as single-minded as the tight-rope walker.

"I'm getting it," he said, dropping to his knees and squeezing under the reporter's table, which began to move.

"Charlie... " Tim hissed.

But he carried on.

Old Outie Tootie had yet to reach the Lord's Prayer, having introduced an appeal to the Almighty to grant wisdom and courage upon the people's elected representatives, which had no chance. He was so engrossed that he didn't notice that the press table was moving across the room in front of him on Charlie's back. Tim sat in the middle of the room like a tortoise without its shell.

Everyone else noticed.

Apart from Cllr Mrs Lady Potts, of the fine legs, pert behind and firm, uplifted breasts. She loved to hear the Vicar speak – he had such well-rounded vowels. Her eyes were closed tightly and she didn't hear the sniggering that had started amongst the less refined elements. There was a faint flush upon her cheeks.

Charlie was oblivious to everything. His attention was purely upon the pen, which had, by chance, come to rest between Lady Potts' feet, just a little distance away. He wriggled free of the table, and scrambled forwards.

"Forgive us our trespasses," moaned the Vicar. Lady Potts' lips moved silently in unison.

"Lead us not into temptation... "

Charlie reached for his pen, and then, only then, did his eyes focus on those trim ankles, and follow the delicious curve of her legs upwards.

"Deliver us from evil..."

Lady Potts screamed, shrill as a rabbit with a stoat at its throat, and as her chair fell backwards she collapsed in an ungainly heap on the floor. Charlie's face appeared between her knees. He looked oddly unruffled for someone who had been so close to heaven.

He waved his pen. "I dropped it," he said, to anyone who cared to listen.

"Amen," said the Vicar.

They helped Lady Potts from the meeting.

Charlie returned to his seat unrepentant. The Mayor was livid. He whispered to his clerk, who passed on the message to the chair of pest control, who had a quick word with one of the minor officials.

He was very nervous. "Uh, Mr O'Flaherty... " he began.

"Who are you?" said Charlie,

"Jones, the minute clerk".

"Just a minute," said Charlie, and laughed noisily.

They called the police. They took him into custody. He was no stranger to the cells and slept well, though noisily.

In the morning, Pc Cartwright shook Charlie awake.

"What time does the council meeting start?" he said.

TIM decided to visit the police station to see when they were releasing his mate.

Smithy the dog dragged him through the park, and it was with some effort that Tim managed to coax him away from a tempting Poodle bitch and out on to the street, just a few minutes from the station.

It had been raining.

As they walked along the pavement a black car hurtled straight through a large puddle next to them, covering Tim and his dog in muddy water. Smithy shook himself vigorously which made Tim even wetter.

"You shit!" shouted Tim, and increased his pace as the black car turned into the police station car park.

Supt Blunder was getting out of the driving seat.

"Why did you do that? You soaked us!" shouted Tim.

"What? Are you talking to me? Why are you so wet?" grinned Blunder, enjoying the moment.

Smithy had a sort of lop-sided smile, too. A dripping, wet, don't give a damn, watch-out-there's-a-thief-about smile. He sidled casually towards Blunder.

"You must have seen us," continued Tim. "I suppose you think it's funny to splash puddles over people from your big fancy plainclothes police car."

"I should be careful what you allege. We already have your accomplice in the cells," said Blunder, adjusting his police blue tie that was covered in tiny pairs of embroidered silver handcuffs. "If you want, we can make one more cell… "

He broke off. There was an unexpected warm feeling around his ankle. It was not unpleasant, a bit like accidentally dipping your elbow into a cup of tepid tea, and it made him look down.

Smithy smiled up at him. The dog's back end was raised up on one leg, and he was peeing with some gusto – a large enough quantity of fluid indeed to have lasted him all the way around the park twice on a normal occasion – on to the bottom of Blunder's police-issue trousers.

"Call him off!" he shouted angrily, whirling away from the dog.

"I think he's finished anyway," said Tim. Smithy trotted obediently over to his side.

"I'm going to get someone out here to arrest you," shouted Blunder, He would have done it himself but he had forgotten the caution.

"What for?"

"Vandalism, criminal damage, a dog that's out of control. Whatever. You'll pay for this."

"What about assault with a deadly weapon?" offered Tim. Smithy felt proud.

"You'll pay for this," repeated the policeman, pulling up his trouser leg and exposing a natty knee-length blue police sock with little patrol cars whizzing round it, soaked through to the skin. And with that he hobbled into the station, leaving them alone.

"I'd say that was poetic justice, wouldn't you?" said Tim, patting the dog.

But by this time the dog wasn't really paying attention. His thoughts were back in the park, with that pretty poodle..

IT was a gloomy May morning. The over-optimistic proprietor of an esplanade amusement arcade, having stayed open after the Easter weekend hoping for a rush of holidaymakers, put up his shutters at 11am and went home to bed, his only visitor having been an Icelandic yachtsman who wanted to know the way to Sydney.

Charlie was bored. He had been down to court to pick up a page lead or two, but the only cases the magistrates heard were TV license dodgers, and there was no copy in that.

He had come to work on the bus because his van wouldn't start again. He had joined the AA but after being called out six times in ten days they banned him.

As soon as he got on the bus a thin man in a dirty mac, gaunt of cheek and hollowed eyes, turned towards him and said: "Good morning."

"Bit wet," Charlie replied.

"The Righteous bathe in eternal sunshine," said he.

The man said he was going to the library, but it was obviously too early and Charlie – who was a great believer in first impressions – identified him as a bible pusher. He presumed he would be dawdling, handing out religious pamphlets, and chastising the ungodly. He was right. The man's conversation became tiresome. Charlie tried to ignore him.

It was, in fact, an ungodly hour, too early to be interested in anything, as far as he was concerned, although a small blonde with a tear in her tights, just above the knee, relieved his from his lethargy for a few moments. And then she got off.

The bible pusher turned his attention to a small, plump, woman with a worried expression and a nervous neck twitch – an altogether more promising target perhaps.

The man behind kept coughing in Charlie's hair and the seat in front had a broken back. A fat woman got on and headed straight for it. When she sat down the seat back pinned his knees down.

"Would you mind moving?" he asked.

"Move yourself," she snarled.

By the time he had extricated himself the bus had passed his stop and he had to walk back.

IT was the day before the Spring Fete and agricultural show... a "fete worse than death" as Charlie put it. Traditionally, Charlie reported the event. He had become so bored by it that he always copied the story from the previous year's, so he only had to change a few winners' names.

After work, he went up to the farm to watch his dad preparing Polly for the pig classes. Arthur had borrowed Charlie's last bottle of after-shave and rubbed her all over with it, dabbing some under his arms as an afterthought. Polly was in ecstasy. It was a smell she adored, and it was all around her.

Every now and again Charlie coughed sharply. Arthur was unmoved. On the pig farm, Charlie's worst was no more than a drop in the ocean.

"Bring her up lovely, this will," cooed Arthur, massaging the pig's hind quarters. "Makes all the difference to the judges, seeing the animal all clean and healthy."

Andrew arrived on his bike.

"I think you ought to stop doing that," he said. "I know no-one believes me, but I think it's the after-shave bottles that keep exploding."

Charlie carefully picked the bottle up and smelt at it.

"You're not kidding us."

"No, it really is dangerous. I think it blew up Sgt Watson's car, the dog van, and the Sandown Queen. There was a bottle in my uncle's bag when it exploded and damaged the train."

Old Arthur took the bottle from him.

"I've been shot in the Trossacks and blown up at Dunkirk. I saw what happened to the train. Maybe you have a point. I think I'll just pour some on this rag to finish Polly off, and then put it somewhere safe," he said.

He tilted the bottle – "It looks Ok, just a nice smell and a bit of froth... well, a lot of froth... "

His voice suddenly changed. The mixture was foaming out from under the cap and dripping onto the ground, where it sizzled and smoked.

"I think you should put that down!" said Andrew's voice from behind a wall.

Arthur looked around frantically. The last thing he wanted to do was blow up his prize pig. No, that was the second to last thing. He wanted to save himself for Molly.

"Throw it down the loo!" shouted Charlie.

Charlie used his dad's loo as a waste disposal unit. It was always blocked by empty cigarette packets and fish wraps.

Arthur hurdled the wall of the pigsty – not bad for a one-legged war veteran clutching his testicles – and dashed for the loo. The door was open and the seat up, and it looked fully operational. He dropped the bottle in the water, slammed down the lid, pulled the rusty chain and ran for his life.

At first there was only the sound of the toilet gently flushing.

But then the ground began to move.

The force of the explosion that demolished Arthur's loo and cracked several walls of the farmhouse sent a shock-wave through the sewer system.

Just off-duty and looking forward to the following day's fete, Beryl Bloggett was at her home on The Broadway. Just as she was settling down in her toilet, reading a copy of Women's Own, a fountain of filthy water rose from the bowels of the earth and tossed her through the wall and into the living room, where she lay, shaken and bruised, in an ocean of raw sewage. At first she blamed the curried beans she had consumed at Mr Patel's Curry House that lunchtime, but when her wits returned to normal she realised that was, of course, impossible, and she had, in reality, been the victim of the Great Serpent of the Sewer.

The ambulance that collected her also called at the farm to pick up Arthur, who Charlie had scraped up from under the toilet door. Badly winded, he still managed to claim: "I told you that stuff was dangerous."

Supt Blunder was disappointed. Told of the explosion, he had hurried to the farm. He had expected to find the bodies of two principal subjects, Charlie O'Flaherty and his dad, and possibly that of their accomplice Sid Pugh.

Case closed.

Instead, he heard wild allegations about an explosion in the sewers from the already discredited nephew of the police chairman, and from the completely unreliable Charlie, as well as the rantings of a evil-smelling and demented woman with her uniform tucked into her knickers who was fighting to get out of the ambulance, apparently because of an imminent second-wave attack by a dragon.

He stood for a few minutes watching a big pig. It stood and watched him. Charlie watched them watching each other. They seemed comfortable with one another. Blunder bent forward and stroked Polly's snout. She bit him. It seemed to Charlie to be justice as it was intended to be seen.

"I need your help," said Andrew in the newsroom later that day. Charlie, Tim and Annie listened and tried to understand. "I once caught an eleven pound cod off Scapa Flow," said Phil the sub.

They ignored him.

"So you are saying that this after-shave you found in the pier pavilion is seriously unstable and has caused all the explosions. So there's no bomber. Is that right?" asked Charlie.

"It is. And the police don't want to know."

"So how many bottles are left?"

He said there were 'about' four – some still in the pavilion, and the one his mother had given to Beryl Bloggett to be put up for sale on the Cats Protection League stall at the spring fete.

"I thought Mabel had that bottle for safe-keeping?" said Tim.

Charlie shook his head – "No, Arthur told me that the bottle was back with Beryl. I presume she will be out of hospital and well enough to run her stall."

"What have you done about the bottles in the pavilion?" asked Annie.

"Nothing. The council closed and guarded the pier because of the damage caused by the Sandown Queen. That part of the pavilion is still roped off. Anyway, the room at the back of the pavilion was locked up last time we were there."

"So it seems sensible, if the police won't do anything about it, for us to buy back the bottle your mum gave to the fete, and keep it safe." said Annie. They all agreed.

Andrew was delighted. At last someone was taking him seriously.

LATER that evening a shadowy figure in a boiler suit and balaclava eluded the security guard at the pier steps (he was distracted as he tried to get his torch to work) and broke-in through a window at the rear of the pavilion, scrambling through the old boxes and packing cases looking for a shelf by the window. It was there, covered in dust, and with marks where bottles had stood. But it was empty.

CHAPTER 19

CAME the great day, and it was raining.

Pc Cartwright was pleased to see the rain because it meant a small crowd and fewer hooligans throwing wet sponges at him on the Knock A Policeman's Helmet Off sideshow. Last year had been dreadful. Supt Blunder had promised to make sure no-one threw foreign objects at him, as they were likely to do, but he had been deliberately distracted by a buxom wench who asked him to help her get a bee out of her bra. Whilst the officer's attention was diverted down her generous cleavage, a burly youth hurled a giant sponge soaked in dye at the unfortunate constable, knocking his hat off and colouring his hair, face and neck navy blue for the rest of the week.

"Well, it does match your uniform," commented Blunder, coming up for air.

The lad demanded a prize but slunk off with the busty girl when threatened with arrest.

The sideshow was the sort of challenge that suited Charlie, with his unfortunate record of police assault, but this year he would be too busy working.

"It always bloody rains when it's the fete," he moaned, sweating in an old anorak and waterproof leggings. He had to take note of the prizewinners. If you missed any out you got a rollicking from old Iron Balls. Prizewinners sold papers. People liked to see their names in the paper. It wasn't so bad getting the results of the vegetable and flower classes, because there weren't many of them at this time of year. It was the cattle and dog and horse jumping events that took the time, wandering through the mud and crap, water down your neck, notebook all soggy. The only consolation was the beer tent.

This year it was out of bounds.

"We don't want any mistakes," said Annie, who seemed to have taken control. "We have to make sure we get that bottle of after-shave before anyone else, and get it to a safe place. Then we can get it analysed properly and be in a position to clear up the cause of the explosions once and for all."

"Surely I can have one pint?" said Charlie.

114

"Not until afterwards. We have to be there at the Cat Protection League stall when the fete opens, and in numbers."

"My uncle is also after the bottle – he needs it to keep his hair growing. Mind you, it's a funny colour. Sort of brown and green," said Andrew.

"What about those still on the pier? Shouldn't we alert the authorities? Or at least try and get them to a place of safety?" suggested Tim.

"I think we should forget about those for a while. The bottle at the fete is a more likely target," said Annie.

Tim said he would bring his car (for once is was working) up to the wall of Sandown recreation ground, ready to receive the bottle, and that Annie should then come with him to the old firing range on Culver Cliff where there were still some bunkers.

"We can put the bottle in there, one of us standing guard while the other fetches the bomb squad. They'll know what to do."

Annie said she would stand guard. Charlie asked Andrew to stay with him to get the story of the fete. By that he meant Andrew could get winners' names while he reported on activities in the beer tent.

They were all unaware of the drama already unfolding.

Arthur had been up since 5am putting the last minute touches to Polly, prior to assembling for the judging of the best sow (three years old) class. But there was a snag.

No-one noticed anything unusual as the pigs were unloaded and assigned their positions in the pig tent, apart from the fact that Polly was covered from snout to tail in an old horse blanket. When Arthur took it off the other competitors gathered around in stunned silence. Someone fetched the Pig Society secretary, and he summoned the judges into an immediate emergency session.

Arthur made the best of a difficult situation.

"It's a breakthrough in breeding," he said. "After years of research I have developed the perfect hybrid pig, ideal for lean meat but also useful if you want to knit a hairy green jumper."

Polly wondered what all the fuss was about. She had never felt so warm and comfortable in her life. It had been a shock to discover upon waking that she was covered from head to trotters in long, green hairs, but they were soft to lie on and kept out the draughts.

The fete opened on time, at 11am. But the Cat Protection League bottle stall remained closed and empty. The Chronicle team had expected someone else would open it in the absence of Beryl Bloggett, again hospitalised, but the only person in the vicinity was Harry the printer. He cleared off as soon as he saw them coming.

Tim brought up the car and they discussed the options. Charlie wanted to break into Miss Bloggett's home, assuming she had the bottle of Heaven Scent there. But Annie urged patience – "I expect someone else will be here in her place," she said.

Charlie decided to be patient in the beer tent. The others hung around.

"Isn't that your Daphne and her sister?" said Andrew.

It was. They were escorting a group of Brownies towards the main show ring. Jemma was their Brown Owl. They saw Tim and both turned their heads away.

"She's not my Daphne. We just liked playing Scouts and Guides," he said.

Annie giggled.

Tim saw Sir Humphrey's Rolls Royce arrive, but didn't take a lot of notice. His mind was on Jemma. As they walked away she half-turned once, but one of the little girls was pulling at her skirt, and the moment passed.

Sir Humphrey had a particular reason to be at the fete. He was worried about Dorothy. She had seemed very distant from him in recent weeks, particularly in the bedroom department. Only the previous night he had sensed a lack of response as they made love.

In the morning, Lady Potts had turned to him and said: "I was so tired last night, I must have dropped straight off. What were you saying?"

"Not a lot. We made love twice," he grumbled.

"Did we, dear?" said her Ladyship vaguely. "Well, I'm sure it was very nice."

Sir Humphrey wondered if he was losing his sexual attraction. He was particularly worried about his hair, which seemed to be thinning. He was determined to buy the bottle of Heaven Scent from the Cat Protection League stall and give his scalp a vigorous massage with it. More hair, even green hair dyed brown, plus a nice perfume, might rekindle the fire in Lady Dorothy's loins. That's if ladies had loins.

The Chronicle team had drifted away from the charity stalls.

Andrew called them back – "Look, it's my aunt. She's doing the cat stall," he said.

Indeed she was. There were already quite a few people, mostly admiring males, standing around as Lady Dorothy spread out the bottles. Pc Cartwright – who also had a passion for Lady Dorothy – made the mistake of proceeding up to the stall from a southerly direction, unobserved by all except Lady Dorothy's dog Poo Poo, which promptly broke its tether and climbed up the constable's leg.

The news team could hear his curses but were screened from witnessing the incident by an ice cream van and the backs of several small children, who were watching with considerable interest.

Lady Potts saw Charlie. "I'm not going to serve you, Mr O'Flaherty, so you might as well go away," she said, obviously still harbouring dark and secret thoughts about the assault in the council chamber.

So did Charlie.

"I can only apologise. It was a misunderstanding due to exhaustion, as a result of having to work such long hours for your husband," he said.

"Nonsense. You are clearly some sort of sex beast. I still wake up thinking about it."

So did Charlie.

There were bottles of all shapes, sizes and colours, containing everything from brown sauce to aspirin tablets, whisky to cough mixture. There were even a few bottles containing perfume and after-shave.

But there was no sign of the bottle they were after.

"My mum donated a bottle of Heaven Scent... do you still have it?" asked Andrew. "It was green and... "

"I know the one, Andrew," interrupted his aunt. "I'm sorry, but it's not here. My husband was kind enough to purchase it as soon as we unloaded Miss Bloggett's trailer. He gave me £5 for it, which is, as you know, very generous."

"Does he still have the bottle on him?" enquired Annie. "We do have a particular reason for wanting it."

"I expect so, you might find him over near the pig tent. He was there a few minutes ago talking to that awful 'Arry – sorry, I mean Harold – Hawkins. Apparently, there has been some sort of commotion, involving – though I can hardly believe it – a relative of Mr O'Flaherty. It must run in the family."

"What's dad been up to now?" grumbled Charlie, as they headed towards the tent.

There was no sign of Sir Humphrey, but Arthur was sitting in the middle of the tent with an arm around his pig. "It's a sit-in, a protest at the fact that they've disqualified her," he said. The officials were ignoring him, carrying on judging, but a small crowd of curious spectators had gathered to watch.

Polly was an incredible sight, her whole body covered in thick green hairs. You could hardly see the skin underneath, apart from on her head.

"That's the only place I didn't rub your after-shave. It must be something to do with that. You should never have suggested it – now I'm a laughing stock."

"It was you who wanted it," argued Charlie. "Must be some sort of biological reaction."

The man from Pig News was taking photos. The Chronicle reporters should have been contacting their own photographer – it was a good story after all – but Tim couldn't be bothered, what with trying to find Sir Humphrey to make the bottle safe, and needing to talk to Jemma.

He would have been even more anxious had he known what was afoot a few hundred yards away, in Sid Pugh's ice cream van. Yes, Sid was there, wearing a natty trilby and dark glasses as a disguise, deep in conversation with Red Harry, who's long trench coat was dripping all over the carpet.

"Old Potts has the bottle, so I'm going to grab it from him," said Harry. "You make your way to the Town Hall steps on foot and

I'll meet you there later, and hand it over, just in case anyone is on to me. You can keep it until we are ready to take it to London."

"But is it safe?" said Sid, nervously remembering his recent encounter with Heaven Scent. His wounds had still not healed.

"It is if you treat it with respect. Don't bounce it around. I'll wrap it in something soft while we are on the move."

"Can I have a cone mister?" said a small voice.

Sid peered over the edge of the counter. A small boy held up a 50p.

"Cones are a pound. Piss off," he said.

When they were alone again, Sid said: "But what about my ice cream van?"

"I'll drive it to the Town Hall, stupid. Then you can take over."

So Sid pulled his trilby down around his ears, turned his collar up, and went out into the rain. No-one was going to identify him in this downpour. Anyway, he had only seen one policeman, and he was busy playing with a dog.

"I've got my pound, Mr Pugh," said the urchin, just as Sid stepped out.

"Sorry, gone up. Two pound now," said Sid, and he vanished into the mist.

The robbery was over in a few seconds.

It was Jemma who found Sir Humphrey, face down in the mud.

Tim heard her cries for help, and was yards ahead of the next man. They gently turned Sir Humphrey over and wiped dirt out of his nose, and away from his eyes. There was a cut and discolouring on the left side of his head, just above the ear. Tim cradled his head on his lap.

Sir Humphrey had been unconscious, but was now coming round, and trying to say something. It was the first time Tim had been close enough to him to get a good look at his hair. It was not quite brown, more rust coloured, and there was a faint green tinge to it. Very odd.

"What happened – did you fall over?" he asked.

"It wasn't like that," said Jemma, quickly. "He was attacked - a man in a long coat was crouching over him, but he ran off. You didn't see his face, did you, Sir Humphrey?"

Tim looked into her eyes. Dear, warm, soft, eyes. He loved that woman. He wanted to take her face in his hands and kiss it.

He reached for her, dropping Sir Humphrey's head back into the mud.

"Mind out, Tim," she scolded, avoiding Tim's lunge, and reaching to support Sir Humphrey. "You have to be more careful. Now he's all muddy again."

"Big dick," murmured the newspaper boss.

"He means that stick," explained Jemma, pointing to a broken off branch lying in the grass a few feet away.

"Did he steal anything, uncle?" said Andrew, anxiously. "Did he steal that bottle of after-shave?"

Sir Humphrey nodded vigorously.

"Big dick," he repeated.

"What's so important about the bottle?" asked Jemma. The rain was trickling down her face, and a few strands of wet hair clung to her forehead. She blew a drop of rain off the end of her nose.

"I love you."

"Do you?" she said, and she reached forward to kiss him, quite forgetting Sir Humphrey's head which plopped back into the mud.

Pc Cartwright arrived, having been released from the clutches of his doggy pal, the animal's lust satisfied. He felt used and abused, discarded like an old, chewed bone.

They explained what had happened.

"And you say all that was stolen was a bottle of after-shave? Bit weird, isn't it?"

"It was a particularly important bottle, my young shaver," said Charlie, "in so much as it contains an explosive mixture that has already wreaked havoc in the town, noticeably amongst members of your own organisation. You were warned, but chose to ignore it."

Pc Cartwright giggled. He felt a bit hysterical. He had cramp in his leg and was wet through to his underpants because of the rainwater that dribbled off his helmet and down his neck. It had been a humiliating morning. He didn't want to go to the sideshow, where there was already a long queue. All he wanted to do was go back to the station, or even better, back home. And now Charlie O'Flaherty was repeating a mischievous story that had already been laughed around the station.

"Well, what are you going to do about it?" demanded Sir Humphrey, sitting up, muddied from tip to toe, and beginning to regain his senses and pomposity.

It took the young officer a moment or two to regain his composure. And then his police training kicked in.

"I shall call out my superintendent. On the face of it, we have here a case of mugging, obviously thwarted by the arrival of the young lady" – he indicated Jemma – "which prevented the thief from taking your valuables. My superiors have already told me that the significance of the after-shave had been considerably over-emphasized by the gutter press."

"We have never printed a word about it," Tim said quickly.

"I should think not," said Sir Humphrey. "It's balderdash. The stuff's a good hair-restorer, but that's the end of it. Exploding after-shave? Pure fantasy."

Pc Cartwright and a lady from the St John Ambulance helped him back to his Rolls, explaining the circumstance of his injury to Lady Dorothy, who cried buckets of sympathy. Well, a thimble full.

The reporters wandered round the showground, looking for the suspect. The rain was beating down but Tim held Jemma's hand and life was wonderful.

It was Andrew who spotted him.

"There's a chap in a long coat looking very furtive behind one of those ice cream vans," he said.

At that moment, the vehicle began to move. It turned slightly towards them and they glimpsed a shadowy face in dark glasses. A single upraised finger gestured in their direction, before it gathered speed, sliding away through the mud.

"Cheeky bastard!" said Tim and Charlie in unison.

"Where's your car?"

"Too late for that, let's follow him in the other van," suggested Andrew.

The key was in the lock, but just as they were about to start it, Pc Cartwright turned up.

"What's going on – are you lot into nicking ice cream vans now?"

They explained what we had seen – "If we don't get after him now, he'll get away, and you will never know who attacked my uncle," said Andrew.

"Then I shall commandeer this ice cream van in the name of the police," said the officer.

He leapt into the seat and drove off, Charlie and Tim in the back, urging him on. Jemma and Andrew wanted to go but there wasn't the room.

It was something of a shock for Harry, struggling to master the controls, to discover another ice cream van in hot pursuit. He could see a policeman in full helmet at the wheel.

Harry's vehicle mounted a pavement and hit a wheelie bin, which careered across the road, narrowly missing his pursuers.

Harry had by this time found third gear and was getting up a full head of steam. The grinding cacophony of I'm Forever Blowing Bubbles was roaring for the vehicle's loudspeakers, sending dogs into spasms of fury all the way up the road. He didn't know how to turn it off. Next to him, on the seat, the bottle of Heaven Scent lay snugly wrapped in one of Sid's mum's knitted pullovers, a trickle of foam spreading out of the cap and into the wool.

The vehicle was shuddering and bouncing and fumes were spreading through a rusty hole in the floor, fogging up the windows.

Pc Cartwright raced through the gears, but couldn't get close enough to identify the driver.

CHAPTER 20

SID Pugh stood at the bottom of the Town Hall steps waiting for Harry. He felt a bit conspicuous, water pouring off his hat, but he didn't want to take shelter in case Harry missed him.

The only other person out in the rain was the traffic warden he had stolen the uniform from. Fortunately, she hadn't recognised him.

Beryl Bloggett was just out of hospital, and determined to put her run of bad luck behind her. The best thing to do, she decided, was to get right back out there and do the job she liked best, and the one that gave her most satisfaction – handing out tickets to disgruntled motorists. It would take her mind off her own troubles.

Beryl gave Sid a suspicious look as she passed – she was tempted to give him a ticket for loitering – but he kept his collar up and started a tuneless whistle which made her edgy, so she carried on.

Sid was on the verge of giving up and going back to his hiding place (the shed at the bottom of his mum's garden) when he heard the sound of his ice cream van's signature tune.

Harry had managed to gain a slight lead going up the hill, handicapped as his pursuers were by having three up, but he knew he didn't have time to stop when he saw Sid waving at the edge of the pavement. He waved back. Sid stepped forward into the gutter and was bowled over by the slipstream as his ice cream van bounced past. He ended up sprawled on the sidewalk with a twisted ankle.

His left arm hurt. But he could still move his fingers. He flourished them at the departing vehicle.

What was Harry up to?

Sid got to his feet, confused and shaken.

Another ice cream van was approaching.

"What a fool I am – it must have been the wrong van," thought Sid. He hoped that no-one had seen his mistake. Good old Harry. He should have known he wouldn't let him down.

Sid stepped off the pavement with a smile on his lips...

Harry had nipped into a side street, waiting for his pursuer to go past. Nothing happened. With the engine turned off the chimes had ceased. It was very peaceful.

Something must have happened to the ice cream van that had been chasing him. It might be a good time to go and collect Sid. He decided to walk, as the Town Hall was not far away, and the police might be looking for the van.

When he got there, two ambulance men were scraping Sid's flattened remains off the tarmac. There was a big dent in the front of the ice cream van that had been pursuing him, and the windscreen was smashed.

Pc Cartwright was sitting in the ambulance in a state of shock, and two other policemen were trying to find witnesses.

Tim saw Harry and went over.

"Terrible business," Tim said.

"Was that Sid Pugh?"

"Yes, it was. How did you know? There's not much of him left."

"I recognised his pink socks," said Harry.

At that moment there was a massive explosion a few streets away. They felt the ground shake. The sky was full of smoke and tiny particles of debris.

The policemen ran towards the area of the blast, just as a frail and tattered figure staggered around the corner.

"It was another b-b-b-bomb, another b-b-b-omb" cried poor Beryl Bloggett, who had been approaching Sid's ice cream van, illegally parked in a resident's only zone, ticket at the ready, when the bottle of Heaven Scent – shaken up by Harry's crazy driving – exploded.

The police, of course, could find no trace of the driver.

Harry quietly slipped away.

They sat Beryl in the ambulance next to Pc Cartwright, who hadn't spoken since the accident, and was shedding tears over the remains of Sid Pugh. She was amazingly composed considering her narrow escape.

She beckoned to Tim as he stood at the open door.

"That's h-h-him who s-s-stole my uniform," she said, pointing to the body under the blanket.

"Pink socks?" he asked

"Pink s-s-s-socks," she said.

"ALL I saw was a flash of his socks on the pavement and then there was a nasty bump," Pc Cartwright told the inquest a couple of days later.

"What sort of bump?" asked Sir Humphrey, the coroner, living up to his reputation for asking completely useless questions.

Pc Cartwright considered the question carefully.

"It was a big bump... like running over.. "

He paused, determined to get it right.

"Yes, go on... "

"Like running over a man."

"But you did run over a man."

"Yes, Sir"

Sir Humphrey whispered to his clerk– "Why is he saying it was like running over a man? There's no doubt, is there? This is the Sid Pugh case, is it not?"

James James, the clerk, stood up and moved closer. "If I may interpret, Sir. He is merely saying what sort of bump it was. It was a bump proportionate to the running over of a man, rather, than, say, a frog."

He sat down well satisfied.

"Where does the frog come into it, and what was he doing driving an ice cream van on the pavement?"

James James groaned inwardly and stood up again. He was fed up explaining to the old fool. There had already been enough evidence from independent witnesses, like Charlie and Tim, for everyone to be clear on exactly what had happened to Sid Pugh.

Pc Cartwright heard the coroner's remark and interrupted.

"The ice cream van wasn't on the pavement, Sir. I saw a flash of his socks on the pavement – that was what I noticed. His socks. Then he stepped off the pavement in front of me and I hit him."

"You mean he was standing in his bare feet? In pouring rain? Was he mentally disturbed?"

James James sighed.

"The socks were on the man, the man was on the pavement, and then the man, in his socks, walked off the pavement and was flattened by Pc Cartwright."

Pc Cartwright gulped, and choked, not having heard it put quite so bluntly before. He sat down, wiping his eyes with a police handkerchief (it was white with blue edges and had little patrol cars all over it).

"So it was a deliberate act, that no-one could have prevented?" said Sir Humphrey, who was getting confused by the whole thing and wanted to be at home in the arms of Fluffy Rabbit. If she'd have him.

"Indeed," said James James.

"But why should the officer deliberately run him over? Didn't he like him?"

Pc Cartwright buried his head in his hands.

"Murderer!" shouted Sid's mum from the back of the court.

James James knew he had to be firm. He stood up and approached the coroner. – "The deliberate act was that of the deceased, in walking into the road in front of the ice cream van. Pc Cartwright had no chance of avoiding him. He cannot be blamed in any way."

"So you think it was suicide?" said Sir Humphrey.

"Mr Pugh was a wanted man. His own ice cream van was demolished shortly after his demise, probably by a bomb he had been carrying for future use. One can only speculate on the reason he walked into the road. I suggest that the evidence is unclear, Sir, and your verdict must reflect that."

"Then why didn't you say so earlier, and saved us all a lot of trouble?" said Sir Humphrey huffily.

And he wrote quickly on the certificate of death, signed it with a flourish, and rose to announce "Open verdict" to the assembled throng. And then he went home for tea and crumpet. He hoped.

A BREAKFAST TV CREW, aware that Beryl Bloggett's name was becoming increasingly familiar on lists of casualties associated with the Sandown bomb blasts, decided to interview her live in hospital.

She was introduced as Bomb Blast Beryl.

"Have you always had bad luck?" asked the interviewer, a petite blond.

"Well, trouble d-d-d-does seem to f-f-follow me around," replied the traffic warden. She had developed a nervous stammer.

"Oh God!" whispered the producer to his assistant.

The interviewer struggled on, determined to see it through. Her reputation was at stake.

"What about childhood accidents? I understand you broke several bones at different times."

"I was in and out of h-h-h-hospital like a yo-y-y-y-y"

"Yo?"

Miss Bloggett nodded, gratefully. She was holding a photo of her cat under the bed clothes. Her psychiatrist had advised her to keep something familiar close by, to reassure her at times of stress.

"And I s-s-s-suppose that's why I h-h-have always b-b-b-b-been lone-l-l-y, because p-p-p-people didn't w-w-want to be n-n-near me if anything h-h-h-happened."

The interviewer edged slightly away, and looked around nervously for the nearest emergency exit. She decided to wrap it up quickly.

"You have been so close to death – finally, can I ask you, is there anything that has given you comfort over the years, and as you lay here today, wondering what fate holds in store for you?"

Beryl smiled – "I thank h-h-h-heavens for m-m-my p-p-p."

"Parents?" interrupted the interviewer.

"p-p-p"

"Priest?"

"p-p-p"

"Pets?"

"P-pussy" said Beryl, and she sighed with satisfaction, and vigorously stroked the photo of dear old Ginger under the blankets.

The camera crew were mortified. Four million viewers didn't know whether to laugh or pretend not to notice. The cameraman – who had remained unmoved by exploding mortars in Korea and a charging rhino in Botswana – was so shocked he lost his balance and stepped sideways, dropping his camera and colliding with the chair the soundman was standing on. The sound man fell across the bed into the arms of the interviewer, for whom he had always felt a deep attachment.

That would have been it, but for the fact that the blond had always regarded herself as much too good for the soundman, and in twisting desperately away from his clutches, she grabbed for the bedside curtain and brought the curtain rail crashing down on to her head.

The famous TV interviewer lay stunned on the floor next to the camera, which happily focussed on the fact that she was wearing the cameraman's Y fronts under her pretty green dress, while he, indeed, was secretly feeling very dainty in a pair of her red briefs. But that is another story.

Miss Bloggett was unhurt, which was unusual for her, but unfortunately her TV appearance upset the police committee, in the form of Sir Humphrey, who suspended her from duty on the grounds that her national exposure had made the traffic warden force a laughing stock.

"What's so unusual about that?" Tim said.

He and Jemma were cleaning up the bedroom before he went off to work. Under the bed, Smithy chewed happily on her tights.

"It's totally unfair to suspend her, just because she's accident prone. Can't you do a story in the Chronicle about it?"

He explained there was no chance of that, with Sir Humphrey directing the newspaper's policy.

CHAPTER 21

Greg took Charlie to do a story and take photos of a local farmer who had left a message saying he had developed a product that would put the Isle of Wight on the map.

"What's it all about?" said Greg.

"Not sure, as long as it has nothing to do with bottles of after-shave."

It didn't. Well, bottles, but not of after-shave.

Neville Gordon was a short, fat, chap, with a weathered face. "It's going to be huge in the inner cities," he said proudly, leading them into the farmhouse, and, as they entered the kitchen, with a sweep of his arm he went on "and there it is."

On the table was an assorted collection of bottles containing a slightly yellow liquid.

"What is it, urine?" said Charlie, disappointed.

"My God, what's happened to it?" said the farmer. "Someone has filled the bottles."

"Charlotte!" he bellowed.

A teenage girl with freckles, long lashes and curly, dark hair dashed in. "What's up, Dad?"

"What have you put in my bottles?"

"It's my dandelion and bean wine. Why, shouldn't I have filled them? They were just standing there empty."

"They weren't empty, they were my latest creation... Isle of Wight Fresh Air, bottled in the countryside with a breath of the sea. That's my slogan and I think it's a winner."

"Oops, sorry," laughed Charlotte. "I thought they were empty."

Charlie was deeply attracted to her. "I'm Charlie," he said, "and this is my photographer Greg."

The photographer extended his hand. He was reluctant to let her go.

"Anyway," said Mr Gordon, "I have some more bottles of the stuff in the barn, with labels on. You'll love them."

He hurried off. "Watch out for Horace, he's in a funny mood," shouted Charlotte after him.

"Who's Horace?" said Charlie.

"Our bull. In the yard. He's usually easy to handle, but today there's some new heifers around and he's a bit excitable."

They looked at the bottles.

"I like the sound of the wine better than the fresh air," laughed Charlie.

"Try some, but I warn you it's lethal stuff."

She fetched three glasses and they sipped the wine. Charlie liked it a lot, and had another, Greg was busy talking to Charlotte, so Charlie sneaked a third. It was strong stuff; it made his head whirl, but Greg was driving.

"Where's your dad?" asked Greg.

She looked worried – "Yes, he's taking a long time, maybe..."

"Help, help... " a shout from the yard, followed by a scream.

Charlie led the charge outside. Mr Gordon was pinned against a wall by the biggest bull Charlie had ever seen. It was roaring with anger and trying to butt the farmer.

Without thinking, Charlie climbed a metal gate and was about to jump into the yard when Charlotte stopped him – "Be careful, take this, it's fully charged."

She handed him a cattle prod.

"Try and distract it, while I get him out!" shouted Charlie.

He leapt down into the mud... and was immediately confronted by the bull, which had turned away from Mr Gordon, who sank down to the ground holding his chest.

Horace charged at Charlie who, bogged down by the clinging mud, couldn't do much to avoid the beast. He lurched to one side, was clubbed by a heaving rear flank as the bull dashed pass, and weakly waved the cattle prod towards its rear end. There was a flash and an even louder roar, this time of pain, and Horace collapsed onto its side.

"Quick, Charlie... " Greg was there by his side, to help him up and out of the gate, where Charlotte had already dragged her father, before slamming it shut.

The bull was back on its feet, the little red eyes glaring angrily at them through the bars.

They called an ambulance for Mr Gordon, who had bad bruising to his side and chest but no obvious major wounds.

"It's thanks to you, Charlie, that he's OK," said Charlotte, giving him a peck on the cheek.

"You were very brave," said Greg.

"More pissed than brave, I think," admitted the hero of the hour.

"And what a great shot, a bulls-eye even; aiming the cattle prod like that – 9,000 volts through the testicles would bring tears to the eyes of a rhinoceros!"

"Ouch!" said Charlie solemnly, reluctant to admit that it had been simply a stroke of luck.

Just before they returned to Greg's car Charlie had a quiet moment with Charlotte.

"What about coming out for a drink – when your dad's better, of course."

She hesitated – "Well, I'd love to really, but it wouldn't be quite right at the moment, would it?"

"Why not?"

"Well, with Greg just having asked me out as well. I'm going to the pictures with him on Friday. You're just a bit too late, sorry Charlie."

That damn Greg. And he'd missed taking any action photos of the rescue; too busy chatting up Charlotte, the sod. Just my luck, thought Charlie.

But he forgave him over a pint at the Frog and Trumpet. And when they went back later in the week to do a story for the Chronicle, Greg took a nice photo of Mr Gordon with Charlie pointing ('You know how the editor hates pointing pictures!' said Charlie gleefully) at Horace, who was still limping.

HERO REPORTER SAVES FARMER FROM SEX–CRAZED BULL said the headline.

Very tasteful.

IT was Mabel who persuaded Arthur to apply for the job at the undertakers.

"You need a proper career, with superannuation, income tax, a health scheme and a mortgage, all the comforts of the modern society, not a dead-end job like you have at the moment. I like a man with prospects and responsibilities," she said.

Arthur thought about it, and after a while it didn't seem so bad.

He could still keep Polly; the other pigs were not so important to him. It was true he was not burdened with the trappings of the modern bureaucracy, never having paid tax or national insurance, but at the same time he had never claimed dole or welfare. He had always felt it was a fair arrangement.

Why the Inland Revenue had never bothered to contact him was uncertain, although it may have had something to do with the fact that they couldn't find an inspector brave enough to face the stench.

So he wrote himself a glowing reference from the Lord Mayor of Dublin, referring to his "vast experience" as the Mayor's chauffeur, which was a slight exaggeration for wasn't the truth of it that he had only once driven any other vehicle than the pig lorry and that was when he was drunk and fancied a spin in a corporation dustcart.

He reasoned that driving a funeral car wouldn't be much different.

He shaved and washed and changed his underpants, and went for an interview at the Avenue Road office of Denton & Denton in his best suit.

Mr Denton Jnr of Denton & Denton was impressed by the O'Flaherty reference. Nevertheless, he didn't like the look of the O'Flaherty leg. "What's wrong with it?" he asked, as O'Flaherty sat before him, the leg stretched out straight.

"Sure, and isn't it a bit stiff," said Arthur, underplaying it a bit. He had adopted an Irish accent to make the reference sound genuine.

"But doesn't it affect your driving?"

"Not that I know of, begorra," said Arthur, which was not much less than the truth, for how could he know if he could have driven any better, never having used two legs?

So Mr Denton Jnr said he could start straight away, as they were particularly busy, with the influenza knocking down the old folk like skittles, particularly at the Corporation Old Folk's Home which had now been sold to private ownership, putting up the charges to such a degree that many of the poor old things lost the will to live (or so Charlie maintained).

Mr Denton Jnr was himself particularly busy, rushing out to measure the wealthy owner of the aforementioned home with a new suit (Denton & Denton was also a gentleman's outfitter, which suited them admirably, providing the opportunity to size up prospective customers for one business whilst measuring them for the other).

"You can go and collect a customer, and take him to St Saviour's Church," said Mr Denton, passing Arthur a scrap of paper with an address written on it.

"What's his name?"

"Oh, Pugh."

For indeed if it wasn't the late and hardly lamented Sid Pugh who was in the process of being given the Grade One Denton & Denton satin-lined oak and brass handles treatment, though the incident meant nothing to Arthur, who didn't follow the papers. Sid's mum had insisted on a laying-in-state in her living room for several days.

The hearse was one of those plush jobs, long and sleek and designed to whisper discreetly along the road. Arthur took the wheel, accompanied by three coffin bearers. He revved without mercy, and his false leg kept slipping off the clutch, with the consequence that the vehicle coughed and farted and bounced its way to Sid's house.

"What's wrong with you?" snarled the head bearer.

"Weak petrol," said Arthur.

Sid's mum was sitting next to the coffin, eating a jam sandwich. They shuffled in. Arthur was not used to the respectful silence. He said hello to Mrs Pugh, for wasn't she his cleaner, but he found it all a little awkward and didn't associate her with the deceased.

"I never knew the late Mr O'Pugh" he said at last.

They all scowled at him.

"Pugh" whispered the head bearer.

Arthur wondered if he should have changed his socks.

He knew his way to St Saviour's Church. It was right next door to Mabel's butcher shop. There were several policemen outside watching the mourners in case they included any obvious fellow-conspirators ("What do bombers look like?" Sgt Trueman had asked, having a cynical side. "You'll know them if they turn up," said Blunder, which was a nice get-out.)

Arthur was unnerved by their presence. He had never been comfortable in the company of policemen or insurance salesmen. He was so taken aback that he drove straight past.

"Stop – you've missed the church!" shouted the head bearer.

Arthur stopped. The tyres screeched, and the coffin fell out of the back (Arthur had not secured the door properly) and as it hit the ground the lid came off (Arthur wasn't much good at screwing either, but don't tell Mabel).

The deceased, in his best high-heeled boots and aquamarine socks lay sprawled in a disgruntled state, half out of the coffin, one leg in the gutter. Fortunately for onlookers he lay face down, for his features had been considerably re-arranged by the impact with the ice cream van, and this latest calamity had not improved them.

There were those in the crowd who came out of affection for his mother (any man of whom might have been his father), and they stared, hypnotised in horror.

Arthur reacted quickly. "I'll see to it, " he said, leaping from the hearse, anxious to make amends, and keen to impress Mabel, who was waving a bloodied knife from the crowd.

He went to the body and grappled with it, intent on returning poor Sid to the privacy of his coffin. The deceased was reluctant to go along with the plan, in fact completely inflexible as far as motivation was concerned. One protruding elbow caught Arthur on the nose and a swinging boot brought tears to the eyes of the head bearer, who was bending to pick up the lid. None the less Arthur would have battled on and succeeded, had his leg not fallen off.

He tumbled back onto the road and stayed there, looking vacantly at his empty trouser.

A platoon of constables marched forward in step, and roughly manhandled the remains of Sid Pugh into the coffin. Someone fetched some nails and the lid was hammered back into place with a Size Ten heel.

As the bearers (augmented by two police volunteers because of the incapacity of Arthur and the head bearer, who was still trying to get his breath) carried the coffin into the church, Pc Cartwright was dispatched to take Arthur into custody.

"What for?" said Arthur, indignantly.

"Disturbing the peace, body stealing, indecent assault... take your pick."

He pulled on the pig man's arm – "Come on, up you get."

"I can't. My leg's come off."

They both looked around.

"Where is it? Are you sitting on it?"

"No. Last time I saw it, it was by the coffin. Then your chaps came along and tidied up."

Mabel appeared, absent-mindedly waving her cleaver, pushing her way roughly through the crowd. Several people had to be attended to for minor wounds.

"Your leg's in the coffin... one of those policemen put it in. I saw it distinctly. I waved and shouted but I wasn't able to get through to tell him because someone next to me fainted. Blood everywhere, must have been her nose, I think. Most odd."

Pc Cartwright called for the assistance of a colleague.

"Escort the prisoner to the police station, while I go and retrieve his leg," he said.

The service was in full swing.

Rev Ootwhistle was nearing the end of his sermon. It was full of moral messages, for hadn't Sid just "followed his conscience" in conducting the alleged bomb campaign, and wasn't he just a "victim of the restless fabric of society?" Mrs Pugh sobbed noisily into a union jack handkerchief in the front row. She was dressed in full colour "as Sid would have wanted" – a pink suit, yellow shoes and a green hat.

Pc Cartwright slipped in by a rear door, and hid behind a curtain near the pulpit.

"Pssst," he hissed as the Vicar approached the alter on his own.

Rev Ootwhistle recognised him as the officer who had driven the ice cream van that had flattened the deceased.

"You most probably are," he agreed. "I know you have been under strain, but you shouldn't drink on duty."

Pc Cartwright didn't know what he meant. But he persevered.

"I say," he said, a bit louder.

The Vicar was on his knees, leading the congregation in prayer.

"What is it? What do you want?"

"There's a loose leg in the coffin."

This time the Vicar was confused. He knew Pugh had been in an accident but he hadn't realised the injuries had been so bad.

"What happened to the rest of him?" he whispered.

To the congregation it appeared as if he was engaged in deep, spiritual contact – lips moving, face uplifted to the heavens. It was far from the truth.

"It fell off outside. I need it back or else he won't have a leg to stand on. I left him out there sitting on the pavement."

"I thought he was dead!" said the Vicar, forgetting to keep his voice down. "So why are we having a burial service? You can't go to all this trouble just for a leg! Whatever next? We'll be burying people's appendix and bunions, or anything that happens to drop off!"

"It's a miracle!" shouted Mrs Pugh, clearly hearing what he had said. "My Sid lives! He's back from the dead. Allelulhiah, and get the port out! He may be minus a leg, but the Lord has sent him back!"

It took some time to sort out.

Mrs Pugh insisted on the coffin being opened, just a crack so she could be sure her Sid was inside, dead, but in one piece, although not in the figurative term. She was helped back to her Pugh, sorry, pew, by the Vicar, while Pc Cartwright fumbled inside trying to sort out Arthur's leg.

It took him three attempts, and he could only manage it by eliminating the late Sid's legs by means of counting them, leaving them hanging outside the coffin for a few moments. It was a horrific sight. Several members of the congregation fainted, and Mrs Pugh – shouting "body snatcher" and "pervert" – had to be restrained. With the false limb safely under his arm at last, he banged the nails back in with his truncheon and faded back behind the curtain.

"Any problems?" said Supt Blunder, who had been outside the whole time.

"I don't think anyone noticed," said the young constable.

ARTHUR was warned about his future conduct, but not charged. Charlie picked him up from the police station. He was still minus his leg because Pc Cartwright had bent it slightly as he forced it out of the coffin, and had taken it round to the hospital to be repaired.

So Charlie went round to pick it up next day.

He found a young doctor using it as a golf club, putting a small white object into an upended waste paper basket.

"That's no way to treat a war hero's leg," he said.

The doctor was unrepentant.

"I've just gone round the room twice in 38 shots. Watch that basket... "

He neatly chipped the white ball into the basket. Charlie looked down at it. A false eye stared blankly back.

"It's just a question of practice," said the doctor modestly.

CHAPTER 22

IT is somehow fitting that Red Harry picked up a red haired girl named Ginger (a graduate of the Home for Wayward Girls) on the fringe of the town's Red Light district.

Actually, Sandown doesn't have a prostitution problem. There's just one tiny back street massage parlour, but local legend weaves a fantasy around the whole area, just like it did when a High Street men's outfitter employed a chap called Bogo who constantly stood in the doorway whistling at passing young men. "He's only being friendly," said Lady Potts, who had had a sheltered upbringing.

Anyway, Harry went straight from Sid's funeral (he kept well in the background) to a pub, to toast the memory of his late mate, and just happened to meet Ginger there.

She invited him back home. "I bet you're not ginger all over," he said as they walked the few hundred yards. She winked at his wit and peered coyly over one shoulder at him as he fondled her buttocks. As one does.

They walked past Honk Pi's curry house, the pavement ankle deep in discarded food plates and paper wrap, an empty litter bin lying bent into a U-shape in the middle of the road. Gallantly Harry steered his companion around the pile of puke that marked the distance it usually took for 12 pints of lager to chemically react with Mr Honk Li's Special Tandoori Hot Pot. The pile of sick was always there; occasionally it changed colour.

No sooner were they indoors than he started to strip her. "Hold on," she said. "Take it easy. Give me a bit of space and I might surprise you."

So he followed her upstairs where, after an exchange of money, she left him on the bed under a fluorescent light while she disrobed in the wardrobe.

When she came out into the darkened room all he could see was a green triangle, just below waist high, which floated around the room and eventually descended onto the bed next to him. The room was full of a clinging scent, like lavender and rose petals.

"Pretty, isn't it?" said Ginger, in her huskiest voice.

"How on earth did you get a green beaver?"

"It just happened. One night about a week ago they just turned green. It doesn't hurt, or irritate. The punters love it."

Harry turned the light on to get a better look. Purely in the interest of science. And then he realised their significance.

"You've been using a new scent, haven't you... called Heaven Scent?" he said.

"It's here," she laughed, "how did you know? It's actually supposed to be an after-shave, but I just splashed it all over like this... "

And she started to sprinkle the noxious fluid on her stomach, and rub it into her pubes, which would be interesting in most circumstances. But Harry was distracted.

"I didn't think there were any bottles left," he said, his voice rising in excitement. "It could be worth a lot of money, but you have to be very careful with it. It could explode."

Ginger laughed.

"Don't be so boring, you old fuss pot. Come on, you have some, let me rub it in... " and she started to wrestle him over onto the bed.

"Stop it!" said Harry, anxiously, trying to force her back, and as he flung out his arm, his hand caught the bottle and sent it flying through the air, over the bed, high towards the ceiling, and down, down, towards the bare boarded floor.

There was a green flash. The explosion blew in the walls of the massage parlour next door, scattering beds and bodies in all directions. Old Iron Balls found himself locked in the embrace of the Director of Piers, Parks and Pubic Places, where seconds earlier they had each been finding fulfilment with a far more attractive partner. Well – let's not exaggerate the charms of these women – a bit more attractive. As mentioned before, times is hard, you don't get much for a quid.

Thrown together by fate, the two men would always remain firm friends.

But of Harry and Ginger and the bottle of Heaven Scent there was nothing left, just a faint green mist hanging over a pile of rubble.

"THAT's eight bottles blown up, now," said Andrew next day, "and I reckon that leaves only one. Bogey agrees with me – there were nine on that shelf. We took seven, and one by one they have been accounted for. Now there's been an eighth explosion. Someone must have been in the room on the pier, and taken the last two."

They were in the Chronicle newsroom writing up the events of the past week. TWO DEAD IN BLAST screamed the front page headline, POLICE BAFFLED BY NEW BOMB TRAGEDY.

"Poor Harry," murmured Annie, "he was just an innocent victim."

"Hardly innocent… " said Tim.

"It's a right mess down there," said Charlie, just back with some eyewitness accounts. "Two houses completely destroyed, the massage parlour wrecked and a chimney pot that landed 80 yards away in Mr Honk Pi's deep-fryer. They had to take him away with fat burns. The place was a foot deep in tandoori."

"How many were injured?"

"Ten, altogether, although the police refused to give me names for two of the customers at Lil's place. Said it might embarrass them, and they had suffered enough."

"Yes, she's a bit rough with the punters. Or so I've heard," Tim said, quickly.

Annie gave him a dirty look.

"Blunder has had to re-open the enquiry, and recall the anti-terrorist squad," added Charlie.

The squad had been sent back to London after Sid's death, because Blunder had the idea that Sid was acting alone, a bomber with a chip on his shoulder, although it was obvious to everyone that he hadn't the intelligence to blow up a balloon let alone a train and a couple of police cars.

"I wish the police would believe us," said Andrew. "We could sort it out right away, before the ninth bottle explodes. Or maybe it has already – there seems to have been such a lot of damage this time that maybe the last two bottles went up together. Or perhaps it's just getting more volatile."

"Do you think Harry had the bottles, or was he just in the wrong place at the wrong time?"

Andrew nodded – "He was a very shady character, and he went around with Sid Pugh. Maybe they were looking for the bottles, but why?"

"Why, indeed?" said Annie. "We'll probably never know."

Meanwhile, events took a most unexpected turn.

Jemma had been busy organising a protest among local students at the suspension of Beryl Bloggett. They were a passionate lot, with a natural sense of justice, and when she explained what had happened they took to the streets. Many had already seen the TV interview that had caused all the trouble, and Beryl was rapidly becoming a cult figure.

"BRING BACK BERYL," shouted the students, gathering with placards outside the police station.

"B-B-B-BRING B-B-B-BACK B-B-BERYL," chanted the more imaginative ones.

At first sight there was nothing unusual about them – they were sloppy, hairy, over-excited and smelt of beer. And that was just the women.

But then Tim noticed something,

"Is that weird, or what?" he asked Jemma.

"What are you talking about?"

"That girl over there – she's got green underarm hair."

"Disgusting that she has hair under the arm at all. Very unhygienic," said Jemma.

"Actually, I quite like a little bit of underarm hair on a woman."

She scowled at him.

They were distracted by a renewed outburst of chanting. Superintendent Blunder had made the mistake of opening a window to look down upon the throng. An egg burst on the window sill and spattered all over him. He ducked back inside.

There was a huge cheer from the crowd, and the beaming marksman was congratulated from all sides.

When they looked around for the girl with green underarms, she had gone.

Next day, Andrew came in late. "I've been to the doctor," he said.

He was a bit embarrassed, but it transpired that he, too, had been having a problem with body hair.

"I've got these green hairs coming up on my chest. And Bogey says he started to get green whiskers, although they went when he used his mum's electrolysis on them, and so far they haven't come back."

"Let's have a look, then," said Annie.

So he undid his shirt, and there they were, a thin mist of green.

"I sprinkled some Heaven Scent on my chest, and Bogey used it on his chin. But that was weeks ago."

Charlie was unusually quiet.

"Have you had any ill affects, Charlie? You used some of it before you gave it to your dad for his pig. And remember what happened to her."

"Well, just an odd green hair, here and there... but my dad's got a load down his back."

ANNIE and Charlie walked to the canteen for lunch.

"There's a sexual side to everything we do or say," observed Charlie.

"No there isn't."

"There is, you know. It's a sexual tension that hangs around us like an invisible cloak, affecting our behaviour and judgements."

She paused and looked at him.

"There's no sexual tension between us."

"There could be."

"Give it up, Charlie. It's a lost argument. You may see sex in everything, but it's not there."

She carried on walking, with Charlie behind.

"It is from where I'm looking," he said, admiring her rear.

"Oh Charlie, what are we going to do with you?" said Annie, exasperated but not angry.

"For starters, I'll settle for a steak and kidney pie" said Charlie.

CHAPTER 23

THERE was some good news for Beryl Bloggett, fresh out of hospital, and sitting around bored at home. The police committee gave her a job. Not her old job, because that would have been admitting defeat, a slap in the face for Sir Humphrey. But they wanted to make a concession to public opinion so they arranged for her to have a position with the recently privatised police forensic department.

"She'll be analysing evidence, blood, sperm, the usual stuff. Dead easy. No training needed. Twenty pounds a week," the department head explained to Supt Blunder.

"I thought you used qualified people, graduates, scientists and micro-biologists?"

"Oh no, those days are gone. If they aren't busy I get them cleaning the windows and washing my car. Works very well."

Beryl was not very happy, but at least it was a job, and hopefully it would keep her off the streets and the dangers that lurked there for the luckless.

She found it hard going.

"I can't type, and I don't know anything about fingerprints and blood tests," she confided to Pc Cartwright.

"Don't worry, I'm sure you'll pick it up in no time," he said.

Meanwhile, Supt Blunder was in an awful mood. His pride had been hurt. The egg stain on his police tunic irritated like an erotic thought in a monastery.

But in his case, it was not too late to do something about it.

To get his own back, he decided to mount a drug raid on the student accommodation.

Granted a few shreds of cannabis were turned up, but the whole exercise – involving five policemen, two dogs and 13 special constables – was out of proportion to the situation, and had it not been for Supt Blunder's eagle eye they would even have missed the after-shave.

"What's that up your nose?" he enquired, of one mild young fellow with far-away eyes, and a stud in his tongue.

"Which nose?" said the student, gazing distantly at unseen horizons.

"In the middle of your face, you idiot. There's something green up your left nostril."

"Could it be a bogey?" suggested the girl who was sharing his bed, not amused at being the centre of interest for the posse of curious policemen who fought for a glimpse of her from the bedroom doorway.

Blunder peered up his nose.

"No, it's green hair. Your nasal hair is all green. Why is that?"

The young man sniffed sharply.

"Don't know..."

"I told him not to sniff the stuff, but he insisted. He's a right sniffer. You've got it, he'll sniff it," said the young woman.

The officer turned his attention to her – "And you appear to have green armpits. Is this some sort of fashion, or what?"

She refused to help. She sulked.

Eventually she pointed out a bottle of Heaven Scent on the shelf above the bath.

"It's that scented stuff. Someone left it here. I'm not sure who."

Blunder examined the bottle. It looked harmless enough. Was this what all the fuss was about? He knew all about the ice cream van chase, the massage parlour explosion and the wild claims made about Heaven Scent by young Bogey Brown and the staff at the Chronicle. He knew he should call in the bomb squad. But he didn't. He stuck it in his pocket and took it to the station.

At the morning press call that afternoon Sgt Wright jokingly announced the drugs haul – "3oz cannabis and a bottle of after-shave."

"What sort of after-shave?" said Charlie, suddenly interested.

"Heaven Scent I believe."

"Bloody hell, we thought it had all been destroyed. That stuff is deadly. You'd better evacuate the building," said Charlie, moving quickly to the door.

"Yes, our young constable has already alerted us to the possible link to the explosions, although I personally think it unlikely," said Blunder. "We are aware of evidence of green smoke and green staining on damaged metalwork, and the young lady who was so tragically killed with Harold Andrews was, it has to be said, covered in green hair in a particularly sensitive area. Or so I'm told."

"Well, what are you going to do about it?"

"I personally took it into custody, and I will deal with it. It is quite safe at the moment, but we won't take any chances."

He instructed Pc Cartwright to carry the bottle – very gingerly and at arms length – into the rear car park, and moved the vehicles away. They placed it in a bucket full of sand.

"That's our sand bucket," said Blunder proudly. "It's for explosives."

"Yes, very impressive," said Charlie. "Look, let me demonstrate the potential danger of this liquid. Just to finally convince you."

"I don't need convincing," said Pc Cartwright, from behind a wheelie bin.

"You can show us if you want," said Blunder, half-hoping Charlie would blow himself up, "just as long as it won't damage my station."

Charlie bent over the bucket and carefully poured a trickle of the after-shave into an old film canister he had in his camera case. Unseen by the officers, he poured a lot more of it into a small bottle and secreted that in an inside pocket.

It was insurance – he was not at all convinced that the Heaven Scent bottle would be safe in police hands. And he had another use for it.

He placed the first container on the tarmac, with the lid on, and suggested to Pc Cartwright that he bash it with his truncheon.

"He might get blown up," pointed out Sgt Trueman.

"True, but only a bit. And he'd get his picture in the paper. I can see the headline now – CONSTABLE DEFIES DEATH TO UNCOVER BOMB SECRET"

"More like POLICE CHIEF SENDS ROOKIE COP TO HIS DEATH," grumbled Supt Blunder. "I hardly think we can take the chance."

"Oh, all right, I'll do it," said Charlie, exasperated. "Pass me your stick."

"Truncheons are police weapons. As a civilian, you'll have to use something else."

They looked around for a suitable bludgeon. All they could find was a bundle of canes tied up in a corner, which Sgt Trueman was taking home for his runner beans.

They were long, but too thin. Not enough clout. But it gave Charlie an idea.

"Have you got a mouse trap?" he asked.

They did. Pc Cartwright fetched it.

Charlie carefully set the spring, and placed the photo canister on its side where the cheese would normally be.

They all retired several yards, and then Charlie leant forward with the longest cane and tripped the trap...

WHOOSH! – The mouse trap skimmed across the ground for several yards with a jet of flame pouring from the canister, rose gradually to a height of 30feet, and then plunged back to the ground as the 'fuel' burnt out, but not before it made a vicious turn towards the startled policemen.

Everyone ducked. Superintendent Blunder was a little slower than the others. It knocked his hat off, and fell to the ground, smoking.

There was an awful smell of burnt hair, and a stunned silence.

"Crikey," said Pc Cartwright at last.

"Impressive, isn't it?" said Charlie, as he bent over the blackened remains of the mouse trap.

"It's burnt my hair," moaned Blunder, clutching the top of his head.

"I thought it was going to fly over the wall, and off across town. And that was just a few drops... imagine what a bottle of the stuff could do?" said the young constable, thoughtfully.

"Imagine... "said Charlie, and he carefully checked the lid was on the bottle in his pocket.

They carried the bottle of Heaven Scent inside in its bucket, and Sgt Trueman called the Forensic Department to collect it. Supt Blunder had the slight burns to his scalp dressed by a young policewoman. She had full breasts that even a police uniform couldn't disguise, and delightful blue eyes. It was almost worth the pain.

The head of Forensic said there would be a three-day delay because of staff cuts.

"We need to get it analysed quickly so we know exactly what we are dealing with. If you don't do it at once, I shall complain to the police committee. They can always cancel your contract," insisted Sgt Trueman.

"Oh very well, I'll set the new girl on it."

"Thank you" said the Sergeant, quite forgetting who the new girl was.

He phoned home and summoned his son and Andrew to the station. They explained how they had found the bottles of Heaven Scent, and what they had done with them.

"We think we left two in the pier pavilion, so it might be them. It might be worth checking there," said Andrew.

"We have. There's no sign of them, just a dusty shelf with marks on."

"Then someone must have taken them. We're not making this up, they were definitely there," said his son.

Sgt Trueman conferred with his superiors. It was decided that a public warning would be issued, coupled with a plea for information

"Hopefully by tomorrow we will have feedback from the forensic department about the chemicals that make up the after-shave. It might help us discover where it was made up, and by whom," said Blunder.

Overnight, there was a break-in at the police station.

"Would you believe we've been burgled," reported Sgt Trueman to his chief next morning.

"What about the security alarms, the patrol dogs and Pc Cartwright on night duty?"

"The alarms were switched off by Pc Cartwright when he went out to feed the dogs. Someone just walked in."

"What did they take?"

"Nothing apparently. Didn't even search the station offices, just tried to get in the forensic lab, but the locks beat them."

Pc Cartwright was carpeted, but otherwise the incident went unobserved and unreported. "Best forgotten," said Blunder.

In the lab, Beryl Bloggett was working her way through 100 sets of fingerprints comparisons, between polishing the windows and washing out the urinals, when her boss arrived with a tray load of test tubes.

"Remember what I told you – just dip the specimen cards in the liquid and wait for the colour change, and then enter corresponding notes in the ledger," he said. "Can you manage?"

Beryl nodded, doubtfully.

She knocked over the first two, and got confused over the colour coding with several others. Nonetheless, she typed in a jumble of numbers and letters, and filed them away.

It was, by now, lunchtime. Beryl had to go home to wash her cat. His name was Henry, he was a blue Persian, and he had been out all night, returning wild-eyed, hair matted and with a cut on his nose early that morning, just as her neighbour was getting his car out to go to work.

"Poor liddle kiddikins, did that beastly she-cat next door have her naughty way with mummy's special darling," Beryl had said, as Henry leapt into her arms at the back door.

"Poor little kiddikins will get a boot up his arseywarse if he stands in my garden howling all night just once more," said the neighbour. "And if my cat is up the spout again, I'm coming round with the garden shears."

"You rude man," said Beryl, and retreated indoors where the smelly Henry was treated to tinned chicken bits and a saucer of warm milk. He lay down for some rest, ready for another night on the tiles.

Beryl hadn't the time to wash him before work, so she resolved to do so at lunchtime.

Just before she left the Forensic Laboratory she noticed her tray contained not only several more test tubes but a bottle of scent of some kind. It looked familiar.

"Heaven Scent," she read...

Ah yes, that was the after–shave that Sir Humphrey's wife had so kindly donated to the bottle stall at the Spring Fayre. What a pity she hadn't been fit to attend. She pulled the top off and smelt it. It was quite lovely, all lemon and cream. It would be just the sort of scent that Henry would wear.

Quite how it came to be in her In tray was uncertain, but its presence there was obviously a mistake, and anyway she would bring the bottle back. She'd only need to use a little of it.

Henry was more reluctant than she expected. Perhaps it was his sixth sense, but he acted as if the very last thing in the world he desired was a rub down in Heaven Scent.

But Beryl persisted. First she trapped him in a corner of the kitchen, then she plonked him into a bowl of soapy warm water, and then she rinsed him from a jar of clean water. Henry slashed at her and raised a bloody weal across her shoulder, but she was made of stout stuff, was Beryl. She held him down with one arm, shook the Heaven Scent bottle, sprinkled some of it into Henry's fur and vigorously massaged it in with her free hand. And then she let him go.

The cat raced round and round the room, making horrible wailing noises, with green fumes pouring from its back. Beryl, dismayed, dropped the bottle, which rolled across the floor and collided with the front door just as the cat was trying to get out of it.

Her neighbour, returning from the office, was just getting out of his car when he heard Henry screeching. "It's that damn cat again," he muttered, and went to open the gate to Beryl's garden, to remonstrate with her.

Except that the gate came off in his hand, and the front door came to meet him.

Heaven Scent

He found himself lying on his back on the bonnet of his wrecked car, with green flames and smoke all around, and a mangled bundle of bloodied, green fur across his clean, white shirt.

CHAPTER 24

THE following day Sup Blunder met his police committee chairman to discuss the latest explosion and the other new developments.

"It means we are going to look pretty silly, doesn't it?" said Sir Humphrey, who was wearing a badly fitting brown wig to hide his green curls, all efforts at dying them a respectable colour having failed. The result was a green fringe around his shirt collar.

Blunder couldn't keep his eyes off it – "Pretty silly, Sir" he agreed. Blunder had been advised not to cover his singed head, but to let the air get to it, with the result that his hair stood boldly up on each side of the flattened area where the flying mouse trap had struck him. He looked like a sort of reverse Mohican.

"We can't tell the press that we have been searching for terrorists when all the time the explosions were being caused by some weird after-shave, can we? An after-shave which we are unable to analyse because it has been taken from out lab and destroyed! I mean, what will they think? They'll get the impression that we are idiots."

"Quite so, Sir," said Blunder.

"But we're not idiots, man... "

"No, I didn't mean 'Quite so' that we were idiots, I meant 'Quite so' that we shouldn't tell them the truth. Not the exact truth..."

THE Sandown Queen had been repaired and relaunched, with a new captain. He was, however, a stranger to the peculiar pulls and eddies of the currents around Sandown Pier landing stage, and on his very first approach drifted too far to port and clobbered the pier just behind the pavilion. It was a shame because the pier had only just been re-opened after the earlier collision.

It caused a dent in the bows and some planking and a length of rail on the pier had to be replaced. But unknown to the council workmen who carried out the repairs, the shock of the ship's collision had also been felt inside the dressing rooms, particularly the smallest, most cramped room of the lot, where the girl dancers usually had to change, until they protested, and were allowed to share with the female impersonator (he flounced about in a fine old fury). And it was in there, hidden from view inside a cupboard, that an old wooden barrel lay, knocked over by the impact. On the side was a label, with the hand-written words 'Heaven Scent - Dangerous chemical. Do not touch.' It was signed Ernest O'Flaherty.

A smoking, green liquid leaked slowly from the bung. Gradually, a sweet scent filled the room, before filtering slowly out of a broken window pane.

"WAS there anything left of that bottle of Heaven Scent after the explosion at Beryl's house?" Annie asked Charlie.

"Not a drop," he said.

"What about at the police station. Did they keep any of it separate, in case of accidents?"

"No, they never thought that Beryl would cock it up, strange though that may seem. She has always been the most accident-prone person in the county, but no-one thought it through."

"So that's it. None left."

"Apparently not, to all intents and purposes," he said, a picture of innocence.

"What does that mean?"

"Nothing."

"You don't seem very sure. Is there any Heaven Scent left?"

"We'll have to wait and see."

Annie looked at him thoughtfully, and then resumed typing.

"Have you seen Old Iron Balls today?" asked Annie.

"No, why?"

"He's shaved his moustache off. He looks really different."

"I'm not surprised," said Charlie. "He spent most of the day yesterday in his office and when he went to the loo he was very furtive. And I know why. I caught a side-view of him in the mirror. His moustache had turned green!"

"Can't think how that happened" said Tim, grinning.

"It must have been somewhere he'd been," offered Charlie, winking.

Later, Annie said: "What you doing tonight, Charlie?"

"Same as always. A few pints at the Frog, then the police press conference, then home to bed. Coming?"
"I will to the pub," she said.

THERE was a good crowd at the press conference, despite the fact that Sir Humphrey called it for 10pm on the assumption that journalists would be reluctant to leave their pubs at that hour. He figured it would be all over before most of them dragged themselves away from the bar.

It also helped that it would be too late to go on the evening's main TV news.

"Hopefully, by tomorrow something else will have diverted their attention – perhaps another England cricketing collapse, or a sex pervert Tory MP," suggested Blunder.

"Steady, you are talking to the chairman of the Sandown Conservative Association," complained Sir Humphrey.

Blunder took command of the press conference.

"After exhaustive enquiries we have reached the conclusion that the probable source of the recent explosions across Sandown is a liquid known as Heaven Scent, an apparent after-shave, but in fact quite a deadly cocktail of substances, including phosphorus," he told the press.

"Preposterous," said Charlie, liking the rhyme.

"Do you mean there never was any bombs?" Annie said, helpfully.

"Questions later," said Blunder, curtly.

"We vant answers!" shouted a voice from the rear. "You cannot stop us, you nasty English pig."

"Crikey, that's a big strong." said the man from the Times, looking round at the elderly, stooped, bearded man with a monocle, standing behind him. "A chap can't go round calling these chaps pigs. Come on, old man, let's play with a straight bat!"

"Don't talk to me about bats, you imbecile," said the old man. "We need to get to the facts. Ver the deaths and injuries, and damage, not caused by terrorists as we ver led to believe? Is there any truth in this rumour about exploding perfume bottles?"

"And who are you, Sir?" demanded Sir Humphrey.

"Von Schweinhund, from Pravda. Stop this pussy-farting around. Ve have ways of making you tell us everything.... everything."

Annie nudged Charlie. "He's not a journalist, he's a Russian spy!"

"How do you know?"

"Oh, uh, well, I remember from when I covered the launch of a space mission, for Today newspaper in Florida. He was part of the Russian team. An ex-Nazi. Space specialist."

Charlie moved quietly over to have a word with Pc Cartwright, who passed the message on to his boss.

"Throw him out," said Blunder.

"But he's an old man. Must be at least 80!"

"Well, that makes it easier, doesn't it!"

So Von Schweinhund, protesting loudly, was escorted to the door, which was then slammed in his face. "Pigs, pigs!" he could be heard shouting.

Blunder's throat was drying up – "We have not exactly ruled out terrorist involvement in distributing Heaven Scent."

"So are you trying to tell us that the IRA have developed an explosive after-shave, which will turn your hair green and gives bald-headed old men a new head of short and curlies? Presumably it's designed not just to kill, but to humiliate and embarrass us. Is that what you are asking us to believe?" Charlie asked.

"Hey, guys, is this the world of fantasy and leprechauns, or what?" laughed Annie.

Sir Humphrey had gone red with rage. He was a colourful picture, red cheeks, brown wig, green fringe. The BBC TV crew couldn't get enough of him.

The cameraman from ITN, however, was obsessed with the two-inch wide parting down the middle of Blunder's hair, and kept zooming up and down it like a jet fighter pilot in the Grand Canyon, before his producer ordered him to stop.

"So as far as the terrorists are concerned, it's a case of 'Hair today, gone tomorrow,'" joked Charlie, never one to let an opportunity pass.

"Isn't this a cover up?" he added. "Is it not true that the police could have cleared all this up months ago if only they had listened to the evidence, and not gone off chasing their own tails. It was one blunder after another, wasn't it, Superintendent...uh... "

"Blunder!" roared several voices at once, as the conference disintegrated into chaos.

Before the chairman and his police chief could respond, Charlie added: "Oh, and how is the hair today?"

"It's fine!" snapped Blunder and Potts simultaneously, and then looked at one another in disgust at having been caught out.

They stalked out of the room, speechless with fury and embarrassment.

It was left to Sgt Trueman to distribute press releases, which called upon the public to hand in any bottles of Heaven Scent that might still be in circulation.

Von Schweinhund made his way to a nearby phone box, patiently waiting while several other reporters filed their pieces. Then he phoned Moscow.

Over the next few days dozens of calls were received by the Heaven Scent hotline, and the police collected hundreds of bottles of after-shave, deodorant, perfume and even sink cleaner.

But not one bottle of Heaven Scent.

There was one important breakthrough, however – the young woman student with the hairy green armpits (sexy green armpits, said Tim) called in at the police station and admitted she had not told the truth about the source of her bottle. She did know where it came from. Her name doesn't matter – the important fact is that she was the daughter of the Chairman of Piers, Perks (sorry, Parks) and Pubic (sorry, Public) Places, and it was he who had given her the Heaven Scent.

"He said it was his last bottle," she said. "He had given another one to a girl he said was a pier dancer."

"Was her name Ginger by any chance?"

The girl said she didn't know.

"He really liked it, said it smelt like rum truffles. He loves rum truffles."

"Seems like it smells different to everyone who uses it. Strange stuff. What chance do we have of sniffing it out," grumbled Pc Cartwright, looking forlornly at his dog.

"It will probably smell like Chum to him," observed Sgt Trueman. "Better leave him at the station. He'll only get confused."

They searched the Director's office, on the pier, but there was no sign of any Heaven Scent. Nor was there any sign of the Director himself.

He had apparently gone away on holiday with Old Iron Balls of the Chronicle

CHAPTER 25

CHARLIE was spending a boring afternoon at his dad's farm, making tea for the plasterer. Arthur had taken Mabel to Whitby for the day.

"Why do I have to baby sit the plasterer?" Charlie grumbled.

"He needs someone to make his tea. He likes it with milk and sugar," Arthur had explained.

"Why can't he make it himself?"

"He'll be busy doing the walls. And his hands will be covered with plaster. Anyway, he's a bit cantankerous. If we don't make him tea, he might piss in the plaster. He's done it before."

So Charlie made the tea, his own special brew.

"It's too strong, and there's a funny acidy taste. Maybe there's not enough sugar?" complained the plasterer. "Your dad makes a nice cup, but this is rubbish."

"I'll make you another," said Charlie. And he did. Just the same, except for a bit more sugar. And he smiled as the plasterer drank every last drop.

ARTHUR bought Mabel a budgie. "It's lovely, but it has a wonky leg," she said.

Indeed it did. Its left leg splayed out and it tottered on its perch.

Arthur took it back to the pet shop and demanded his £2 back.

"No refunds, taken as seen," said the pet shop man. "But we can swap it for another one."

Arthur considered the alternatives.

One had a flat head.

"Why has it got a flat head?"

"It had a difficult birth," said the pet shop man.

"Have you any others?"

"Well there is this one, but there's a slight problem," said the pet shop man, pointing to a pretty blue and yellow bird chirping brightly in his cage in the window.

"Looks great to me," said Arthur, sticking a finger into the cage and waggling it. "Here little bird, pretty boy."

"Fuck off, Vicar," said the little bird.

"That's the drawback," said the pet shop man. "We don't know where he picked it up from, but it doesn't appeal to everyone"

"I'll take it," said Arthur, happily. It would be a sensation if he could get Mabel to invite the Rev Ootwhistle round for tea.

PC CARTWRIGHT went to see Beryl Bloggett in hospital. He had been once before, a few days after the explosion that wrecked her home, but she was heavily sedated and thought he was her doctor, which proved a bit embarrassing as she kept asking him to look at her chest.

This time she was awake. She peered short-sightedly at him, looked worried when she saw his uniform, and then smiled in recognition.

"I thought I would just pop in to see how you are. The lads at the station wanted me to, to b-b-bring you these flowers," he stammered, looking around nervously, poised for a quick exit if an accident occurred. Beryl had that affect on people.

"Don't you start stammering – I've only just managed to stop!" she giggled.

He was surprised how well she looked. Her hair was short, a sort of ragged, elfin-look that emphasised her soft features, and she was wearing a little make-up, which was unusual for her. The thick-lensed glasses were on the bedside cabinet. He hadn't realised that she was only a little older than he was.

She giggled again – "They've made me up, changed my image. It's part of my therapy, you see. I have to believe that the old, unlucky me was destroyed when the house exploded."

"Do you remember much about it?" he asked, sitting close to the bed. He had been in the rescue team searching for the body – he had moved a kitchen table, and saw her arm move. He would never forget it.

"Oh yes, every bit. I was so relieved to see you. I was frightened the house would catch fire and burn me alive."

A nurse took away his flowers to find a vase. On the bedside cabinet was a basket full of fruit and chocolates.

"Someone has given you a nice gift."

"No, you are my first visitor. That's a raffle prize. The nurse came round with tickets and I won, believe it nor not. The first time I have ever won anything."

"Maybe your luck is changing."

"My psychiatrist says I have to think lucky. He says no–one can have the misfortune I suffered permanently, it was just a bad run. None of it was my fault, just unfortunate coincidences, in the wrong place at the wrong time. I just have to be extra careful, but confident – watch my feet, and keep my head held high. But obviously not at the same time, or there would be an accident!"

"You must have been in despair at times."

"I was, and I even turned to religion. I prayed a lot but the first time I went to church the Vicar tripped over my handbag and bashed his head against the font, and the next time a little boy in the pew behind was sick down my neck. So I thought it wasn't meant to be."

She reached out and touched his truncheon.

"It's massive. I bet that would hurt someone."

"I expect it would, but I've never had the chance to use it."

"It's a bit bent."

"They all are. Designed like that, but it's still OK."

"Perhaps it's a good job you haven't used it," she said, fingering the gnarled end.

"Well, I would like to, just to see how effective it is."

"Well, maybe you can have a go at me. Just a little bonk. Just to get the feel of it!" she laughed.

"Don't get me going or I will," he smiled.

They chatted for several minutes, and then he said he had to go.

"Are you coming back to work in the lab?" he asked

"For the time being. But it's not my sort of job. I think I'll go into the construction business, get a job in demolition!"

"Seriously... ?"

"I don't know. I'll see. If you have any ideas you can tell me next time you come in. Or when I get back to the lab. Can you do something for me? I have filled in my football pools. Can you post them for me? I think it's about time I tried out my new, lucky life, don't you!"

He laughed, and took the pools entry – "Maybe some of it will rub off on me"

Unfortunately, as he stood up his ankle caught round a trailing cable, which pulled sharply on a drip food holder next to the bed, and it fell forward, giving him a nasty bang on the head.

"Ouch, obviously not yet," he grinned, rubbing the bruised spot.

CHARLIE was sunning himself in a sheltered corner, between the mash boiler and generator.

He was helping around the farm while his dad took Mabel away for a dirty weekend. "This should be you, son, smart young fellow with money in his pocket and oats to sow," his dad had said.

"I think Mabel's too old for me, dad," said Charlie.

Having completed his round collecting pig food, Charlie had boiled up the mess and opened the air valve to send it whistling through the feed pipes. It was a sound that excited the dullest porker. Whatever they were doing – grubbing through the mud, nose up a backside, sleeping, eating, philosophising – ceased at once, as they headed for the food troughs. It was not unknown for a sow to dash across with her piglets bumping from her sides, hanging desperately on, as they finished their delicious milk shake.

Sometimes they got there just before the food. Impatient snouts pushed and sucked at the vibrating end of the pipe, until, as if stimulated into action, the mother load burst upon them: juicy, delicious, streams of liquidised bread, beans, apple crumble, and cauliflower, with the occasional old teabag and sanitary towel to make a bit of roughage.

Only today something was different. Polly did not join the melee. Normally she was at the front, barging her way in, squashed tomato over one eye, custard down her chest. Today she stayed where she was, nose poked through the gate, sniffing towards the sea. The only other time he had seen her off her food like this was the day she strayed on to the railway line.

Charlie stood up. He was about to go in to call the vet when he heard the barking of dogs in the distance, and an exhausted fox burst into the farm yard, where it dashed around in panic, penned in on three sides by pig pens and barns. He heard the sound of the huntsman's horn, and it was obvious what was afoot.

Quickly he rolled back the door of his tractor shed – conveniently empty – and the fox dashed in. He slid it back into place. It was dark in the shed and the fox quietened, just as the dogs burst into the yard.

In seconds he was up to his knees in hounds, leaping and sniffing and wandering about. They completely ignored his pigs, which were huddled up in a corner of their pen, trying to burrow underneath one another in their panic.

More to the point, the dogs had no idea what had happened to their quarry, their sense of smell distracted by a plethora of aromas – pigs, pig food, pig manure, Charlie's socks. Particularly the latter. They barked and whined, and above their din could be heard the thump, thump of the generator and the shrill whine of the compressed air food pipe, still pumping out pig swill. It was a scene of chaos.

"Call off your dogs!" Charlie shouted angrily at the huntsmen, who were just arriving.

Sir Humphrey Potts, Master of the Hounds, rode to the front of his troops – "Not until you show us the fox. We know it's here somewhere."

"This is private land, and you are upsetting my dad's pigs. I want you to leave. Now!" said Charlie, moving over towards the pig trough.

"We don't care about your pigs! They are quite safe in that disgusting pen, filthy swine," argued the newspaper boss. "Just give us the fox and we will be gone."

"Call me a filthy swine, will you, " Charlie muttered. " I'll show you who's filthy... "

And with that Charlie unhooked the pig food pipe, still pouring out a flood of hot mush, and lifted it high in the air, directing the stream of liquidised nasties over the heads of the startled huntsmen.

They fled down the lane, gathering out of range down at the gate to wipe soggy pie crusts, apple cores and sour cream out of their hair, and lemon curd, jelly and coffee stains off their tailored jackets and jodhpurs. Sir Humphrey, his hat dislodged in the scrum, his hair an even more unlikely shade of reddy/brown, the result of a direct hit with a gallon or more of tomato ketchup and congealed gravy, shook his fist, cursing and threatening retribution.

The dogs would have stayed, lapping up puddles of steaming food, had Charlie not taken a piece of plank to a dustbin lid and driven them back to their masters.

It was not for an hour or two, long after the hunt had gone, that Charlie freed the fox. And it was at least 20 minutes later when he discovered that the door to the pigpen had been knocked off its hinges during the farmyard melee, and his dad's beloved Polly had escaped.

CHAPTER 26

CHARLIE lost his job. He was fired when he turned up for work next morning. "Persistent insubordination," snarled Sir Humphrey.

"I'll sue," growled Charlie.

"We'll walk out, go on strike, you can get the newspaper out on your own," said Tim.

"Hear, hear," said Annie.

"You wouldn't dare," said Sir Humphrey.

"Yes, we would, uncle, I mean. Pottsy-Poo. I'm going out on strike with them," said Andrew.

"Pottsy-Poo?" whispered Tim.

"It's one of my aunt's pet names for him," explained the lad.

"To hell with the lot of you" snarled Pottsy-Poo.

"I'll carry on working, Sir," said Phil the sub, showing his true colours.

So they walked out and left him to it.

CHARLIE had a phone call from Mad Maggie at the Irish pub.

"I hear you lost your job. You'd be interested in making some money then. Would you like to bet some real money on the flying machine race, ye heathen scum?" she said.

"You sound pretty confident. You know they've banned hang gliders?"

"Of course. But they won't let you use all those bicycle gears either. So what about a £20 wager?"

"Make it £30," said Charlie.

"That we finish in front of you?"

"No. That we win it and you don't. Otherwise I can see one of your lot sabotaging our machine even before we start, in which case all you would have to do would be to stick on a couple of paper wings and leap into the sea and you would have the grand.''

"Sure and you haven't got a very trusting soul. Not for an O'Flaherty. It comes from living with these English barbarians all these years."

"That's the deal. Both machines have to start, and the winner gets the money."

"Will you come round and seal it with a kiss then, Mr O'Flaherty?"

"Sorry love, it's against my religion."

She laughed. More like a cackle. "See you on the pier, then. Have the money ready."

POLLY had vanished. Quite a trick for a 20-stone green-haired pig. She had been gone two days now, and there had been one sighting, by a paper boy, who spotted her walking towards the river which flowed between Arthur's farm and the sea front.

They gathered at the farm to decide their next move. Tim, Annie and Charlie had plenty of time on their hands now they were on strike. They left Andrew picketing.

"I still think it has got something to do with Heaven Scent. Polly loved it when I washed her in it, and has never quite been the same since. And this week the smell of it is in the air again - didn't you notice it?"

"Don't know how you can detect anything, apart from pig manure and that food you boil up," said Charlie.

Tim knew what Arthur meant – "I kept getting a whiff of something spicy as I left work the other day. It came and went on the wind, from the direction of the sea front. I thought at the time it was from the seaside rock factory, but maybe it wasn't."

"I wish I could stay and help but I have to take some Brownies to the Gang Show on the pier this afternoon," explained Jemma.

Annie said she was helping out there as well.

"You wouldn't get me within a mile of the pavilion – my uncle is going," said Andrew.

"I bet he's the President of the Cub's Association," said Charlie.

"Nope. Lady Dorothy is Grand Owl of the Guides, or something like that. They are both going."

"Well, before you all leave, I have something to show you."

Charlie took them into the barn. His aluminium flying machine stood by the side of stacked hay bales. Light streamed through a hole in the roof, illuminating drifting specks of dust and shining off the chrome handlebars. The pedals had gone, and there was no gear wheel or propeller. At the back of the machine was a rather rough looking steel pipe, one end linked to tubes and a glass bottle under the pilot's seat, the other welded to a nozzle that appeared to have been beaten and folded into shape out of sheets of tin.

"Looks great, doesn't it?" said Charlie proudly.

"If there's no propeller, how does it gain momentum?" asked Tim.

"Rocket fuel," said he proudly. "Uncle Ernest's rocket fuel...."

He told them he was convinced that Heaven Scent was, in fact, an attempt by poor old Ernest to protect his invention. No-one would ever think that a few old bottles in a dusty back room actually contained his secret revolutionary new rocket fuel. He kept it in bottles, disguised as after-shave, until the time came to announce his success to the world, but unfortunately he was killed before that moment arrived.

"The bottles sat there undisturbed until young Andrew and his mate found them, and even after the explosions no-one realised what it was. Not even me. Not until I used some to fly the mousetrap at the police station. If a few small drops could make that take off like a rocket, imagine what a gallon of it could do!" he said.

"Remember we are talking about over 20 years ago, when there was a lot more interest in space travel from the British government than there is now. Uncle's formula might have given us a lead in space exploration, and it still could."

"But how could it, if there's none left? It's all been destroyed, hasn't it?" said Annie.

"Not all of it. A little bit came into my possession at the police station."

"Is it safe? Is it here in the barn?"

"There's enough to get us going, to take our plane further out from the pier than Mad Maggie's machine, so that we win the bet. I have it safely tucked away. But it's not here."

"Do you seriously intend to use it to fly your machine, after what happened to Harry and Sid Pugh?" said Annie. "Wouldn't it make more sense to hand it over to the authorities, just to be sure that no-one else gets hurt? I'll do it, if you are a bit embarrassed about it. And you never know what might happen with that chap Von Schweinhund in town. He'd stop at nothing to get it."

Arthur walked over to the Flying Pig and patted the saddle. "We talked about it, me and Charlie, and we decided that Ernest would have wanted it this way. I'm going to be the pilot, because I'm small and light, and I wouldn't want anyone else to be at risk."

"Are you sure?" Tim found himself saying, "I piloted it last time. I don't mind."

Jemma was looking at him and frowning, as if to say: "What are you doing? Don't get involved you idiot!"

"No, thanks anyway, but dad's going to fly it," said Charlie.

Tim felt hugely relieved.

"If this Heaven Scent is so good, such a breakthrough, then don't you owe it to your uncle, and to your country and the space industry as a whole, to hand it over for analysis, in case it can be copied and reproduced? I'll take it in if you like," said Annie, obviously keen to get it into safer hands.

But Charlie wouldn't budge. "I want to use it for one flight, to justify Uncle's faith in it. If there is any left afterwards, then we might do as you suggest."

"Anyway, from the way Polly is behaving I have the feeling that there might be some more of the stuff lying around somewhere, just waiting to be found. I think Polly is hot on the scent. Find her, and you will find Heaven Scent, if there is any," Arthur confided sadly as they left the barn, the flying machine hidden under a tarpaulin.

"Don't worry. She'll turn up," Jemma said, placing a comforting arm around his thin shoulders.

A FEW hours later there was a rap on the farm door and a man with a green moustache peered into the hall. He wore a dark suit and well polished shoes, and carried a small leather briefcase.

"Mr O'Flaherty?" he enquired.

"Might be.... " There was fear in Arthur's eyes. He knew a bible-basher when he saw one, even though this one was hiding behind a green bush and didn't have any smart-arsed, holier-than-thou kids to back him up. They could, of course, be outside, trying to convert his chickens. He peered around the door but couldn't see anyone.

"Mr O'Flaherty the pig man?"

"Livestock consultant," corrected Arthur. He had been well-drilled by Mabel.

"My name is Parks, Peter Parks. I am the Director of Piers, Perks – sorry Parks – and Pubic, sorry, Public Places. Or at least I was. Until I had an accident."

"Yes, I heard about that," said Arthur.

"I have in my possession something that belongs to you," he continued.

Arthur was suddenly interested. "You haven't found Polly, have you?"

"I wasn't aware that you had lost her, whoever she may be."

"Polly's a pig. Been missing three days."

"You have my sympathies, but no, this is nothing to do with a pig. More about peace of mind."

Arthur was losing patience. "Did you know a girl called Ginger?" he asked.

Mr Parks was taken aback. "A minor associate, perhaps, nothing more."

"I thought you did. From what I hear either your moustache has been associated with her nether regions, or both of you were at one time using Heaven Scent. Is that name familiar to you?"

"Ah yes, Heaven Scent," said Mr Parks, glad that their conversation was focussed at last. "Yes, I do have some knowledge of the potion you refer to, and I did indeed introduce it to the aforementioned Ginger, though I would prefer that remained confidential. It was part of my previous, unhappy, aimless life. I am now a born-again Christian."

"Didn't have anything to do with a flash of light, green light, did it?" asked Arthur.

"Just about the same time you met Mr Ball?" interrupted Charlie.

"You certainly are both well informed."

"My son is a journalist on the Chronicle," explained Arthur proudly.

"And a very fine one I'm sure, but even he will be unaware of what I am about to tell you. That Heaven Scent you mentioned – everyone thought it had all been destroyed, so my daughter says, but it hasn't. I have a barrel of the stuff. Had it for weeks."

"We thought as much! Why didn't you tell the police? There have been warnings in all the papers, and on the television."

"At first I was unaware of the risk, and the unpleasant side effects. I found it hidden in a small room in the pavilion, together with a couple of bottles. It had a pleasant smell, and it seemed to turn on girls like Ginger. After the explosion I realised my wicked ways had to stop, and having become involved in a new, deeper, spiritual relationship... yes, with Mr Ball... I became aware that I had been distracted from my duty. I should have reported the barrel to you."

"But how did you know the barrel had anything to do with me, Mr Pier?"

"Parks, Peter Parks. The barrel has your brother's name on it, the late Ernest. It's still on the pier. When I came back from holiday and found it leaking, and heard from my daughter about how dangerous it is, I knew I had to get in touch."

"Leaking?"

"Toppled over on one side, and leaking from the bung. The room was full of fumes, and something needs to be done about it."

CHAPTER 27

"YOU searched the pier weeks ago. Didn't you check the dressing room area?" crackled the voice of Sgt Trueman on Pc Cartwright's radio.

"Yes, you know I did."

"Well how is that we now have a message from old Arthur O'Flaherty that there's a barrel of Heaven Scent in a ladies loo there? How could it be there, if you searched it?"

"Well, I didn't actually go in to the Ladies... "

"Why not?"

"I didn't like to. You know, being the Ladies. There might have been someone in there."

"So what if there was! My God, you're a grown man, and a police officer. You have the right to search the ladies loo and, if you feel so inclined, anyone you find in there. Now get down to the pavilion, and if there is a barrel of the stuff in the loo you had better evacuate the pier. It's the Gang Show today, so you'll have to be quick. Get everyone out. Close it down. OK?"

So Pc Cartwright broke off his foot patrol, and hastened towards the pier, his head full of visions of bravery, What if he found the barrel, and it was leaking? Maybe he could plug it with a finger? Maybe he could lift it up, stagger to the rail and hurl it in the sea? He could imagine the press coverage. PC's COURAGE SAVES CHILDREN, the headline might read, or HERO PC WOUNDED BY BLAST. Only a small wound, of course. Perhaps even VC FOR CONSTABLE. Beryl would be very impressed.

He was quite unaware of the pig bearing down on him.

Somehow, Polly had at last found a way across the river, and was heading for the pier, as fast as her fat, hairy legs would take her.

Tim, Charlie and Arthur, having driven in from the farm, saw pig and policeman converging.

"It's Polly. Quick, we must stop her!" shouted Arthur.

"Stop, pig!" bellowed Charlie, never one to miss such an opportunity,

Pc Cartwright turned slowly. He hated being mocked by layabouts. He was reaching inside his tunic for his anti-personnel gas spray when he realised he was not the so-called "pig" referred to.

His first instinct upon seeing Polly was to shin up a lamp-post. He had always been unsure of animals. Wild or domestic they always seemed to regard him as their playthings. Scratched by kittens, shagged by dogs, pecked by canaries, the constable generally regretted any contact with them.

He saw the green-haired pig thundering down the road, frothing at the mouth with the ecstasy of the wind-borne aroma, and a newspaper headline flashed before his eyes – PC MAULED BY MAD PIG. But the thin blue line didn't waver. Years of police training came into their own. He stuck out his chest, extended his arms, and blocked the pavement.

The pig stopped. It didn't like the look of Pc Cartwright one bit. It had a vision of a newspaper headline – PIG BATTERED BY MAD POLICEMAN.

Charlie and Tim, puffing hard, joined the pig and the policeman. Arthur was some way behind.

"Is this your animal?" said PcCartwright sternly.

"No, I'm just trying to catch it. It escaped from the pig farm," said Charlie, truthfully.

"Well, I've caught it," said the officer smugly. He could see the headline – BRAVE PC CAPTURES HOG.

"You haven't actually secured it yet," pointed out Charlie, who well knew the difficulty facing anyone who attempted to impose confinement on a 20-stone sow without the advantage of:

* a net
* a fork lift truck
* a bag of bruised apples. Polly loved bruised apples.

Pc Cartwright nervously fingered his truncheon. He wished he had a length of rope. He briefly considered using his handcuffs to keep her under control, but dismissed it. He would have been ridiculed in the popular press, and savaged by Pigs Weekly. He thought about using his police belt (it was white with little blue police motor-cycle patrolmen riding round) but he feared his trousers would fall down. He stood undecided.

Polly had no such problem. She caught a delectable whiff of Heaven Scent, borne fresh on the wind that eddied in and out of the esplanade hotels, and completely forgot her anxiety over the policeman. It was as if he didn't exist. She walked through him.

One minute Pc Cartwright was there, all shiny buttons and pressed trousers (a tribute to the force and his mum's steam iron), the next he was merely a part of the pavement. Comfy underfoot, thought Polly as she trod him under. What a nice policeman.

Charlie, Tim and Arthur leapt over his crumpled body and continued the pursuit.

"Officer down" mumbled Pc Cartwright into his radio, like they did on Z Cars.

THEY lost Polly half-way down Pier Street. She waddled across the road in front of a startled glazing salesman, who braked abruptly, lost control of his van, and collided with Mrs Booth's wool shop. By the time Tim, Charlie and Arthur had stepped gingerly through the broken glass, and parted the gawping onlookers, there was no sign of the pig. "Head for the pier!" urged Arthur.

Polly, meanwhile, had been distracted by an ice cream. A small boy sat on the pavement eating a cornet whilst his mum looked out to sea. Polly liked ice cream. One minute a generous lump of vanilla sat proudly atop the cornet, the next it was gone, and so was the pig.

Tears flowed – "Nice cream, nice cream, t'airy pig ate it," howled the child.

"What pig?" said his mum, looking around.

"T'airy pig 'tol my nice cream," blubbed the infant.

I must do something about the way he speaks, thought his mum. And the way he eats, belting that cornet down. "Don't tell porkies, you must have eaten it!" she shrilled, "and stop wiping your nose on my tights, you're just like your dad."

Polly beat her pursuers to the pier turnstiles by a minute, bursting straight under them.

The young lady who handed out entrance tickets was just about to go after her when Charlie appeared, fumbling for his loose change.

"Three please," he said.

"You can't take a pig on the pier."

"I'm not."

"Yes you are, I saw it. And he's the pig man. I recognise him."

"Quite right," explained Charlie, "we are chasing the pig, because it escaped."

"Pull the other one" sneered the girl, who had a bouffant hairstyle, bright red lips and a pink spotted dress. "Last week I had a man who had green hair. He said he was in the pier show but I knew him. Trying to pull a fast one. And him from the council."

"Must have been Mr Parks," said Tim, suddenly interested.

"Yes, one of those environment blokes. Came round about the smell from the toilets once... it was terrible. I don't know why I stay. They pay rubbish and... "

"No time for that," interrupted Charlie, who was feeling in quite a domineering mood. He quite fancied bossy girls. And he liked her lips. "Well how much is it for the pig?"

"Pigs are banned. And dogs. And cats" – it was an afterthought, but it sounded impressive.

"How about threepence?" asked Charlie.

"Done," said the girl.

"Are you keen on gymnastics?" he asked hopefully.

"What's that?"

"Oh, nothing really. Would you like to come out for a drink tonight?"

"Sod off, spotty," said the girl.

So Charlie followed Tim through, leaving Arthur to pay.

ON stage, the Vicar was doing his conjuring tricks. Most of it was lost on the younger members of the Gang Show audience, who weren't near enough to see the sleight of hand that created eggs out of small boys' ears and bouquets of paper flowers from down his trousers. But they did enjoy the goldfish bowl trick, whereby he plucked fat, juicy goldfish out of their bowl, swallowed them (in fact he left the fish where they were, and swallowed concealed slices of carrot instead) and then pulled aside a gold and red cloth (borrowed from his altar) to miraculously restore the fish to their watery home.

Tim and Charlie had separated to find the pig. On the south side of the pier Tim passed a stack of deck chairs just as Andrew's face appeared from under the cover. "Do you sleep there?" he said.

Andrew was pink with embarrassment. "No, um, I was just having a rest."

Tim could hear a girl giggling inside.

"Have you seen Arthur's pig, you know, Polly, with the green hair? We need to catch her quickly, and I've followed her here."

"That was what I was looking out for," said Andrew quickly. "I heard something sniffing around, and thought it was that police dog. It must have been the pig. It seemed to go off toward the back of the pavilion."

"Sorry I bothered you," said Tim, hastening off.

CHAPTER 28

SIR Humphrey Potts sat in the front row next to the Mayor and Supt Blunder, who was representing the police. There had been wild applause from the packed audience of parents when the Vicar finally left the stage, a stunned silence during a tortuous violin concerto by the primary school Year 6, followed by even wilder applause, which may have been an expression of relief that it was over.

"What's next?" whispered Sir Humphrey.

The Mayor consulted a programme. "Old MacDonald had a farm," he said. "By the infants."

"One can hardly wait," muttered Blunder.

The kiddies looked very sweet in their animal costumes, and sang beautifully. But the sudden appearance of a large pig, lumbering in from stage left, seemed a little over the top for a children's show, particularly when the pig was wearing a green coat and snorting loudly.

"It's that pig man's animal, Polly, been missing for a couple of days!" shouted Blunder, leaping to his feet,

"Arrest it," ordered Potts, who was also Chairman of the Police Committee.

Polly was good with children. She sniffed the air and followed her nose, waddling nimbly between the ranks of singing hens, goats, cows and sheep, and even pausing to lick the face of a startled piglet. In seconds she had crossed and departed stage right.

The Vicar was changing back into his frock in the dancers' changing room when there was a knock on the door. It was Lady Dorothy. "I thought you were wonderful," she said. Her breasts were heaving. He crossed the floor to her.

"It was nothing, just a few cheap tricks. I dedicated them to you. It meant a great deal to me that you were here."

He clasped her to him. His cassock rode up at the front.

"And I wanted you to want me to see you," said Lady Dorothy. "I have been afraid to speak of my feelings, but I cannot hold myself back."

Her dress rode up at the front, too.

"Thank the Lord," said the Vicar, and they collapsed into one another's arms on an unsightly pile of stage props, including a low comedian's whoopee cushions.

There was a rasping explosion.

"I am so sorry, my love. It's becoming a bit of a problem. It must had been the haddock," said the Vicar.

And then there was another.

"It's just a little thing, nothing to worry about," said Lady Dorothy.

I thought it was quite big, thought the Vicar.

The door crashed open without so much as a "How's thine Father?" and Polly burst in.

The great green sow didn't hesitate at the sight of the couple squirming on the floor (and they hardly noticed her). She walked round them, sniffing the air, into the ladies closet. There was a squeal of joy and excitement, and a climatic bellow of triumph. But that wasn't the pig, it was the Vicar.

Inside the Ladies loo all was quiet. Polly had found the oozing barrel of Heaven Scent and was licking the bung.

Meanwhile, Pc Cartwright's emergency call had met with a rapid response from the police station. No, not the flying squad, just Beryl Bloggett on her bike. The station was unmanned, what with Pc Cartwright on patrol, Supt Blunder attending the Gang Show and Sgt Trueman having a dental appointment, and the only person to hear the constable's call for assistance was Miss Bloggett, back at work in the lab. Her little heart pounded with exertion and excitement as she pushed down on the pedals.

She found him where he had fallen, but by now on his knees, head in the gutter, surrounded by a group of curious old ladies fresh from a meeting of the WI, one of whom was poking him with her umbrella.

Beryl fell on him with a passion – indeed with the strength of two burly coastguards as the adrenalin flowed, turning him on his back despite his feeble protests and administering the kiss of life. Despite initial resistance, the young officer relaxed in her arms and she felt the tip of his tongue between his lips. They kissed breathlessly. ""Disgusting!" said the old crone, and walloped them vigorously across the buttocks.

"I was actually in the gutter looking for my whistle," gasped Pc Cartwright when they came out of the clinch.

"Forget it, let's evacuate the pier," ordered Miss Bloggett, suddenly fired with new confidence.

ON stage, the scout leaders were performing their own version of Sandie Shaw's hit 'There's Always Something There to Remind Me', barefoot and in full drag. Some looked as if they were enjoying it too much. Jemma sat with two brownies' mums. She had become as assistant Brown Owl. Tim loved her in uniform.

TIM and Charlie met outside the door to the changing room. Sir Humphrey was also there. "I'm looking for my wife," he said. "She was with me one minute, and then vanished."

"Must have been the Vicar's magic personality," said Charlie, who had heard the rumours.

Muffled grunting noises could be heard from behind the door.

"It could be Polly," suggested Charlie.

Supt Blunder joined them. Tim explained about the dangerous barrel of Heaven Scent, and the possibility of an explosion if Polly found it. Both Blunder and Sir Humphrey stepped back a few feet.

"I'll evacuate the building," said Blunder, and headed back to the stage.

"We must capture the beast," said Sir Humphrey, dramatically, suddenly aware of his standing in the community. "Follow me!"

He swung open the door, nearly knocking down the Vicar who was adjusting his cassock. Lady Potts had her dress tucked in to her knickers but tried to look as if nothing had happened.

"Hello Pottsie," she said. "Is the show over?"

Her husband stood silent, stricken into paralysis.

Tim and Charlie barged past and into the Ladies loo. Polly was lying on the floor, eyes closed, mouth open under a steady drip,

drip of green fluid from the barrel, which was still on the cupboard shelf. The room was full of noxious fumes.

"It could go up at any moment, and take us all with it!" shouted Charlie. "Chuck it out of the window!"

There was one window in the room, which opened up onto the slanting roof of a pier shelter, one of those where old folk find seats away from the wind where they can enjoy sea views as they eat their sarnies, or young lovers carve their initials and steam up the windows on cold winter nights.

It was here that Pc Cartwright and Beryl Bloggett were entwined, having discovered that the pavilion was already being evacuated, and resolving to warn those further towards the pier head of their impending doom. Their good resolve had lasted only as far as the first convenient shelter in which they could re-ignite the fire that burned in their loins (yes, girls must have them). They kissed passionately. The strap of Pc Cartwright's helmet got in the way a bit, but it didn't put them off.

Their moment of ecstasy was interrupted by a massive thump on the roof above their heads, and then a rolling noise accompanied by a voice Pc Cartwright clearly recognised as that belonging to Charlie O'Flaherty, which warned: "If there's anyone below, run for it!"

There was a moment of quiet and then a large barrel landed with a thump on the pier decking, green fluid and smoke bursting from every seam, and careered away from them, spinning towards the railings where it became wedged.

Pc Cartwright broke out of the clinch.

"If that blows up it will kill us and destroy the pier," he said.

"Leave it, let's run."

"I can't. There's no time... I love you."

And he ran towards the barrel.

"I love you too," shouted Beryl.

"Will you... " he started to say, lifting the barrel from under the railing and hurling it over the side of the pier.

"Will I what?"

Onlookers on shore reported a green flash across the horizon, followed by a huge bang and an explosion of water that rose high above the pier carrying planking and other debris with it. At the crest of the wave a policeman's helmet sailed through the air, spinning crazily at first and then drifting down to land on the top of Ernest O'Flaherty's statue, where it perched jauntily on his brow. Somebody cheered. It seemed appropriate somehow.

The blast was so intense that it rattled windows as far away as Arthur's pig farm on the other side of town and could clearly be heard even by the bomb squad, who had once again given up trying to find any explosives and were rattling their way home on the Sandown Express.

Casualties were surprisingly few, apart from in the direct vicinity of the explosion. Ambulances rushed off several children who had been close to the pier and been knocked over by the blast, but they were just suffering from shock.

Lady Potts was brought in to hospital and given a private room because of her emotional state. The Vicar, taken to casualty for treatment to a nasty bruise down his right cheek, was suddenly accosted by an angry mother, firmly clutching a small boy by the neck of his jumper.

"It's all your fault!" she said, slapping Rev Ootwhistle across the face, raising a matching red weal down his left cheek.

"Madam, to what are you referring? Surely you can't blame me for this terrible explosion?" said poor old Outie Tootie, rubbing the new injury.

"Explosion? It were nowt to do with t'explosion," said the woman, "twere your stupid goldfish trick. Swallowing them there fish."

"But, madam, they weren't fish, that was the point. They were slices of carrot. I had palmed the fish and restored them, quite safe and unharmed, to their water."

"Yes, but Aaron didn't know that, did he?" she said, giving the lad a shake. "He went home and swallowed his sister's pet goldfish Harriet and Henrietta, didn't he? She's crying her eyes out and I have had to bring this little devil here, for a check up."

"Oi you!" A woman in a big hat at the back of the waiting room stood up and joined the clamour. "There's two more of us over here, with kids that have swallowed goldfish. And my little Nathan was having a go at a frog he found next to the garden pond when I caught him. There was only one leg sticking out, but I grabbed it in time. The poor thing's leg came off, so we have a one-legged frog hopping about our garden now. You should be ashamed, you a man of the cloth. And I remember you from the bus, you stinker."

"It was all a misunderstanding," bleated the Vicar.

"Like me finding you with my wife. I suppose it was spiritual guidance you were giving her, with your trousers around your ankles!" bellowed Sir Humphrey, hobbling into casualty, his clothes tattered, his face scratched and black from the smoke, his eyebrows singed.

Of his wig there was no sign, although a few days later old Phil was fishing off Lake beach when he hooked a black, bedraggled object which fell back into the sea before he could land it. "It was a giant squid, gave me a hell of a fight, and towed my boat for about six miles before I had to cut the line," he told his pals later.

Tim and Charlie pulled themselves out from under the collapsed ceiling of the Ladies loo and rounded up Polly. They were all covered in a fine layer of dust.

Arthur was waiting with his pig food lorry to take Polly home, She was very quiet. The fire had gone out of her eyes. "Thank God that damn after-shave has been destroyed. It caused a lot of problems. Maybe now Polly will calm down," said Arthur.

Charlie looked at Tim and winked. "Don't forget the flying race," he said.

Arthur shuddered. "Sooner that's over, the better," he said.

Pc Cartwright was washed up a few hours later, a few hundred yards south of the pier.

They thought he was already dead but, just as Beryl arrived, water lapping around her ankles, he opened his eyes and smiled at her.

"Give us another hug," he said.

She did. And he died in her arms.

"The answer was Yes. I would have married you," she whispered.

Beryl was inconsolable, as was Poo Poo. They rushed Beryl to hospital and placed her in her favourite bed. She was singed around the edges but otherwise OK. Somebody had found Pc Cartwright's whistle and took it to her. Occasionally she blew little peeps on it as she gazed blankly out across the sea.

They gave Pc Cartwright a proper police funeral, with lines of Bobbies on the streets and a Union Jack over the coffin. He would have been proud of the Chronicle's front page headline, FINAL FAREWELL TO POLICE HERO. The bomb squad were pallbearers. Beryl, back in her traffic warden uniform, led the parade carrying his helmet and truncheon.

In the absence of Rev Ootwhistle, who had been ordered to take compassionate leave, the Bishop conducted the service. At the graveside, as a police bugler sounded The Last Post (the Chronicle report insisted on calling in The Last Pot) Beryl accompanied it with feeble blasts on his whistle. It brought tears to the eyes.

Lady Potts, who had decided like a good Tory wife to try and make a go of her marriage, accompanied her husband, and led Poo Poo, wearing a black bow, behind the funeral cortège. He (the dog not the husband) waited for an opportune moment and then peed on the wheel of the hearse. It was his own silent tribute.

"THEY made a nice couple," said Charlie, unusually sentimental after the funeral. "They were well suited, it was a shame they didn't have longer together."

"I know what you mean," said Tim. "I'm really glad I found Jemma. I feel settled with her, you know, happy to be in a relationship. It's a nice feeling. They must have had that same satisfaction, although briefly."

"I'd like to be a couple," said Charlie, ruefully.

They were having a quiet beer at the bar in the Frog and Trumpet.

"Well, you'll have to find someone. You will. You're an attractive chap, sort of."

"What do you mean, sort of?"

"Oh, I suppose I mean you're tall and not bad looking, really. Maybe you should drink less, and wear more fashionable clothes, and develop some sort of conversation skills, and do something about the spots, and… "

"Thanks a lot, mate. Anything else wrong with me?"

They stood in silence for a few moments.

Daphne came over. She had forgiven Tim long ago. "Anything else, gents, another pint Charlie?"

"No, I'm giving it up."

She laughed. "That'll be the day. If you stopped drinking we'd go bust from loss of profits."

Charlie didn't respond.

"Are you OK, mate?" said Tim.

"Not really. I feel a bit down. I think I'll go home."

And he walked out.

"Midlife crisis?" whispered Daphne.

"He's not that old, just looks it sometimes," said Tim. "I think it's because he's not getting any… you know what I mean?"

"Poor old Charlie. You should have said. I think he's quite nice, really. And I've still got some of that cream left that you liked. Do you think he would be interested?"

"All his birthdays would have come together," said Tim, smiling.

CHAPTER 29

DAMAGE to the pier was extensive, but restricted to one side. It wouldn't affect the Annual Flying Machine Race – renamed the Pc Cartwright Memorial Race – from the pier head. Annie kept close to Charlie in the days before the race. She insisted on helping him with the final adjustments to the flying machine, and slept overnight at the farm to help guard it. With a £30 wager at stake, plus the £30 first prize, they were convinced that Mad Maggie and her team would try sabotage.

"She's sleeping on a camp bed in the barn," Charlie told Tim, "I lay awake thinking about her. Do you think she fancies me? Should I make a move?"

"Can't do any harm," advised Tim. "But maybe you should wait. Why not have a go at Daphne at the pub? I know she likes you."

Next morning Charlie had a bruised cheek.

"What happened?"

"I'm not talking about it. But I wish I'd taken your advice and waited."

They had a test fire of the new rocket system, with the Flying Pig secured to the ground with thick cables. "Just a few drops," said Charlie, pouring the fuel carefully into the tank from a small cocoa tin. He used a match for ignition and immediately the barn filled with thick green smoke and the Flying Pig rocked and vibrated as it tried to break free. Charlie cut off the oxygen supply with a rubber cap and the engine shut down.

"Not much of a test," offered Annie.

"I meant to do it longer but it was getting out of control. It obviously works, so that's good enough."

Came the big day.

Jemma was worried. She and Smithy were going off to escort the Brownies to their viewing point for the Flying Machine Race, on the esplanade to the north of the pier, but first she needed to know that Tim was not in any danger.

"You are definitely not going to be the pilot, nor light the fuel, that's right, isn't it?"

"I'll be Ok. I just have to give Arthur a push-off and then stand out of the way."

The team wheeled their aircraft along the pier. To be truthful, it didn't look very aerodynamic, you know, not many smooth lines. More like a collection of tea chests wired together, with wings sticking out.

Mad Maggie was already on the pier, sanding down the sides of the Irish pub's machine, The Green Streak. It had a sharp, pointed nose – a bit like Mad Maggie herself – but it was more wings than anything, obviously designed to glide as far as possible. It looked very impressive.

She laughed as they wheeled the Flying Pig past. "To be sure and you haven't got a chance with that heap of scrap, it will fall straight into the sea," she said.

They ignored her.

"Have you got the fuel?" Annie whispered to Charlie.

"It's in my bag. The one that my dad is carrying."

Arthur followed behind. He was wearing a one-piece black swimming costume under long johns, thick corduroy trousers and several woolly jumpers.

"I don't want to get cold," he told Tim.

Tim looked anxiously out to sea. The Sandown Queen was hove-to about half a mile out waiting for the race to end so it could unload its passengers, who were mostly drink-crazed pensioners on a day out from their care homes.

Over a dozen rescue boats were circling nearby, ready to pluck the gallant if foolhardy pilots out of the water. Furthest away, and in most cases indicating a certain reluctance to get involved, were a smaller group. No-one expected a flying machine to reach that far.

One of them was manned by Supt Blunder – determined not to get any spray on his new police tie – accompanied by his new constable, who was already feeling seasick.

Beryl Bloggett was in another boat. She had been so determined to have a new, less accident-prone life, that she had joined the volunteer coastguards. She had a new confidence, born of her brief and unconsummated romance with the late Pc Cartwright.

Her small dinghy was at the very edge of the rescue fleet, not because she didn't want to get involved in any rescue, but because she had been reliably informed by her friend Mavis the butcher lady that Arthur's team were going to beat all the existing distance records, and Mavis had asked her to be there to fish him out when his aircraft landed, crashed or sank, whatever was appropriate.

Knowing her reputation, however, her fellow coastguards were reluctant to join her so she was in the boat on her own.

Sir Humphrey Potts led the remaining coastguards in a motor launch. He was trying to impress Lady Potts with his youthful vigour, wearing full yellow oilskins and a kiss-me-quick hat, but somehow it just looked silly. Poo Poo the dog was with him. Poo Poo stood on his hind legs against the bulwarks and looked lovingly across the sea at the new young constable. He liked a man in uniform.

Phil the sub was out there, too. But he wasn't intending to rescue anyone, just to do some fishing. His little boat had an outboard motor and he steered it out over an old wreck, about 50 yards from Miss Bloggett. He was smoking as he sat, rod in hand, watching his little red float. When he finished his fag he lobbed it in the water and tunelessly whistled a libretto from HMS Pinafore.

The Flying Pig was seventh to go, out of eight. The first three pilots leapt off the pier with shouts of excitement, but their machines went almost straight down into the sea. Fourth away was Mad Maggie. Three burly pub regulars gave her a good start with a long run-up, and as soon as the Green Streak was airborne, it caught an uplift of air and soared rapidly away. The crowd cheered and applauded and even Charlie and Tim had to admit it was pretty impressive. The Green Streak must have travelled a good 300 yards before it finally sank down into the waves, and Mad Maggie, punching the air in delight, was pulled into a boat.

"Right, there's only two to go before us. Pour that fuel in and stand by with the matches. Arthur better get in the cockpit," ordered Tim.

They looked around. "Where are they?" said Charlie.

They had been so engrossed in the progress of the Green Streak that they hadn't noticed that the other two members of their team had drifted away.

No Arthur, no Annie – and no bag containing the last of the Heaven Scent fuel.

Then they heard shouting and banging from behind a door in the kitchen of the Pier Head café. It was locked but they could plainly hear Arthur's voice demanding to be released, and when someone fetched a key the old warrior stumbled out.

"Where's Annie?" asked Tim.

"Where's the bag with the fuel in it?" demanded Charlie.

"Both gone. She grabbed the bag and pushed me in here," said Arthur. "She said she was sorry, but when I fell over I dented my leg. Look."

It was bent into a right angle, so badly damaged that he would never have been able to get into the driving seat of the Flying Pig, even if they had the fuel to power it.

"What about the wager? We're going to lose all that money" pointed out Tim.

"What money, we haven't got any to lose! And I can see Mad Maggie's muscle men taking it very badly when we say we can't pay."

"What's Annie up to? Why has she dumped us like this? Has she been got-at by Mad Maggie's team?"

Charlie shook his head. "I think it's more significant than that. But I'm not thinking about it now. Let's see what we can do to get us out of this mess."

He walked up to the Flying Pig, unscrewed the cap on the fuel tank, and peered inside. He probed around with a stick, inspected the end, sniffed it and then announced – "Well, I think there's at least enough left in there from the trial run to get lift off, so let's go for it."

Charlie looked worried. "I suppose I'll have to be the pilot," he volunteered glumly. "It's only fair considering that there might be a risk with the fuel we are using."

Tim didn't argue.

They strapped Charlie in the seat. There was no time for him to get changed into a swim suit, or even a rain coat.

"Are you ready?" shouted the Mayor.

"We are."

"Then off you go!"

Tim and Arthur, who was not much use hopping on one leg, pushed the Flying Pig to the edge of the pier, and stopped.

"You'll need more of a run up than that, my lad," said the Mayor, who considered himself an expert, and privately could hardly wait for Tim and his ungainly machine to fall into the sea, in revenge for the soaking he had endured at their hands the previous year.

"No we won't," said Tim, as he put a match to the fuel pipe.

The explosion knocked Tim off his feet and the Flying Pig vanished in a cloud of green smoke. The Mayor, who had in his enthusiasm unfortunately stepped a little too far forward, was hurled to one side by the blast and fell into the sea.

The cheers of the crowd on the beach fell silent, perhaps in awe, as a large, lumpy thing with wings, a bit like a badly packed parcel, hurled itself from the pier head and skimmed across the waves. It somehow avoided the main group of rescue craft, but appeared to be on a direct course with the smaller group led by Pottsie and his not-so-brave coastguards.

"It's going to hit us! Full speed ahead and hard a-starboard!" shouted Sir Humphrey to his helmsman, who did just that. Unfortunately, at the very same moment Supt Blunder also panicked and ordered his new constable to go hard to port, which he did, whilst opening the throttle, and within seconds the two boats had collided and everyone was thrown into the water.

There was a gasp of dismay from the crowd but – just yards from colliding with the heaving mass of men and dog struggling in the waves – the Flying Pig caught a sudden updraft from the edge of a squall, and began to climb steeply, higher and higher, until it reached about 1000 feet. And then the fuel burnt out.

"Oh God, the fuels run out!" shouted Tim on the pier.

"Bugger, the fuels run out," muttered Charlie, placing both hands protectively around his testicles, as the aircraft levelled out. Slowly the nose began to drop down. From his vantage point he could see the crowds on the beach, the little group of Brownies with Jemma and Smithy, the parish church, even Arthur's farm, but the horizon suddenly blurred as the Flying Pig gathered speed and hurtled back down towards the sea.

Beryl Bloggett rowed frantically towards the group in the water, keeping one eye on them and the other on Charlie's aircraft as it came rapidly back towards them. The inability to stop her eyes from crossing was one of her less appealing features.

Phil the sub was oblivious to everything. His sand eels bait had enjoyed a couple of nibbles and he was still hopeful of catching a nice pollack. He was concentrating so hard he had half bitten through his ciggy. The screams of those around him who thought they were about to drown fell on deaf ears.

He didn't even hear the whistle of air on tortured canvas and the creak of aluminium struts under pressure as the Flying Pig hurtled down towards his boat. Charlie, who was pilot in name only for he had no way of aiming the machine, braced himself for the crash, but his shift in weight made the Flying Pig flatten out of its dive and turn sharply to port, the front nose cone catching the fisherman's coat and lifting him off his feet. One minute Phil was catching a fish, the next he was the catch, snatched out of his boat and dangling helplessly a foot above the waves. Hoist by his own petard perhaps.

On the esplanade Jemma watched in horror as the aircraft hopped across the waves with Phil dangling from the front and the pilot, whom she presumed to be old Arthur, hanging from his seat, held in only by his belt. It was heading back towards the pier.

The Mayor had been helped from the water by several burly members of Mad Maggie's crew and was being escorted down the pier with a blanket around his shoulders by a St John Ambulance man when to his amazement through the green mist the Flying Pig re-appeared, silently, like a ghostly reminder of past misfortunes. For a moment he thought he was hallucinating, particularly as there was a red-faced man waving a fishing rod hanging from the front, but then there was a huge crash and he was once again thrown into the sea.

Out at sea the rescue was continuing. Beryl Bloggett had hauled several people into her boat, which was so overloaded it was in danger of foundering. "Help me, save me!" screamed Sir Humphrey, grabbing the side, but one of his loyal coastguards banged an oar down on his head and Pottsie let go and drifted away. "He would have sunk us," explained the man. They nodded. It had been the best thing to do.

Other boats were on their way.

On shore, everyone was running towards the pier. Jemma stood with her Brownies, not wanting to desert them but fearing for Arthur's safety. She was under pressure from Smithy who was pulling hard on the lead. Then Annie suddenly appeared. "You go, I'll look after them," she said, calling the Brownies to her.

"I thought you were on the pier?"

"I was, but I had to leave. Go on, quick, they might need you."

So Jemma and Smithy ran to the pier.

Tim was there, frantically tearing at a pile of broken planks amid the ruins of a pier shelter, and so was Arthur, leaning on the rail and looking down at the churning water.

"I thought you were on the plane?" said Jemma.

"Late change of plan. Unfortunately, it's Charlie. We can't find him," explained the old man dejectedly.

There was a groan and then a shout of anger from the middle of the wreckage, and a hand appeared from the smoking debris brandishing a broken fishing rod. "I'll sue the bastards. Look what they've done to me and my rod!" shouted Phil.

Smithy was pulling hard at the lead and trying to bite through it.

"Let him go, he might be able to find Charlie," urged Arthur.

The dog leapt on to the very top of the pile of burnt and broken wood, sniffed the air, and then dashed off back down the pier towards the shore.

Phil's language was getting worse. They left him where he was.

Arthur's vantage point gave him a good view of the beach.

"I can see Smithy – he's running down to the water, under the pier. But now I've lost sight of him."

The Mayor was directly below them, hanging on to a barnacle encrusted stanchion, his hands bleeding, too cold and wet even to call out.

Smithy ran towards him and then started to swim. "Go away, you nasty brute," muttered the Mayor, who had never liked dogs, and was beginning to fall asleep.

Smithy ignored him, doggy-paddled several yards past and took a bite at something below surface. First time he missed, snatching only water, but at the second attempt, his teeth held firm into blue cloth and he turned, dragging a body towards the beach. It was hard work as the waves first pulled him in, and then tried to carry him back out, but eventually he made enough progress to be able to touch sand beneath his feet and get his shoulders into hauling his burden up onto the beach.

Tim and Jemma were there to help.

"Oh Charlie," wept Jemma, as she worked on his chest, trying to pump air back into his lungs.

"Try the kiss of life," murmured Charlie.

CHAPTER 30

AT the inquest into Sir Humphrey's death there was much
evidence about the surprising speed and distance achieved by the
Flying Pig, and how the rescue boats had been caught napping by the
manner in which events unfolded so swiftly. Several men in dark
Ministry of Defence suits were in the front row, and they seemed
particularly interested in Charlie's account of how such a tiny
amount of Uncle Ernest's fuel had achieved such velocity.

Phil the sub gave evidence and blamed the Government for
everything, which wasn't much help. He wore a bandage around his
head, and war medals bought at a local second-hand shop bounced
up and down on his yellow oilskin jacket as his long-suffering wife
helped him to the door.

Beryl Bloggett, who had achieved heroine status in the press
for her initial single-handed rescue of five brave coastguards, a
police constable and the dog which had miraculously attached itself
to his leg, received a round of applause from those present after
stating that she would in future look after Poo Poo now that Sir
Humphrey was gone and Lady Potts had run off to Bognor with the
Vicar.

Supt Blunder gave evidence despite suffering from a cold.
He constantly sneezed in to a dark blue police handkerchief, with
embroidered whistles, but was able to recall how he had clung to his
upturned boat until someone had thrown a rope ladder down from
the Sandown Queen, but, having then fallen from the ladder, he was
plucked from an untimely death beneath the scything paddles by
Miss Bloggett's rag tag crew, who felt that maybe they did have
room for one more after all.

A verdict of accidental death was reached.

Tim breathed a sigh of relief.

"They could have said we were to blame for all of this," he
confided to Jemma.

"You're lucky it's the inquest into Sir Humphrey's death,
and not Charlie's," said Jemma, kissing his nose.

The Coroner paid tribute to Sir Humphrey's long career of
public service (the Chronicle report unfortunately again spelt it

'pubic service') and said no-one would know how it was that he had the misfortune to succumb so quickly to the sea when others had lived long enough to be rescued. Perhaps he had banged his head.

After the inquest the ministry men questioned Arthur closely about his brother's work, but left disappointed that no more Heaven Scent remained. They felt it might have helped Britain's space programme.

The gang were soon all back working on the Chronicle.

With Sir Humphrey gone, Lady Potts had put Andrew in charge and he reinstated Charlie and gave them all a pay rise.

Mad Maggie refused to pay them the £30 wager on the grounds that they had cheated, by using a jet engine. They decided not to argue as she was bigger than they were.

No-one knew what happened to Annie.

When Jemma reached the esplanade after Charlie and the Mayor were rescued (Smithy had reluctantly gone back into the sea to save him also) she found the Brownies waiting for her, but Annie had gone.

"I asked one of the girls and apparently Annie had an argument with a man with a foreign accent, who kept clicking his heels and calling her Anastasia. The man tried to steal her handbag and she punched him on the nose. They ran off in different directions," explained Jemma.

"Sounds like that Russian, Von Schweinhund," said Charlie. "I feel a bit let-down because I think now that she was always after the Heaven Scent, the rest was just a cover story. She was a sort of spy."

"Not after your body then?"

"Sadly not, just my scent. She waited for the right moment and grabbed it from my dad, obviously to take it back to the USA. I doubt we'll ever hear from her again."

And they didn't... well, not for a long time

Life continued as usual. Charlie asked Daphne out but she had just taken up with a burly coastguard and postponed his cream birthday treat.

There were no more explosions, and Beryl Bloggett – full of confidence and no longer accident prone – joined the police force, soon becoming a sergeant. She always carried Pc Cartwright's truncheon at her side.

About a year later, a postcard dropped through Charlie's front door. It was a photo of the first moon rocket launch at Cape Canaveral, and on the back was written in green ink: "Thanks for your help, guys."

There was no signature.

But wasn't that more than just a trace of green in the smoke coming out of the base of the rocket carrying Neil Armstrong and Edwin 'Buzz' Aldrin as it hurtled into space?

CHAPTER THE LAST

CHARLIE found the Sixties, or rather the Sixties found him. But he only just made it.

He was walking home from the pub at his usual time (just after closing) in late November 1969 when a woman appeared in the light of a porch on a rather nice Georgian-style house, and called out "Hello, you there. I've been waiting for you."

Charlie looked around. He was there. No-one else was there.

"Did you want me?" he asked.

"You'll do. You're about his size."

She led him indoors. There was something familiar about her.

It was a very nice house. A woman's touch. Flowers, vases, nice paintings, big cushions, long curtains. A grand piano. Family photos, including one of his hostess at a younger age doing gymnastics. And a pile of men's suits on the pile of the carpet.

"Try them on. If they fit, you can have them," she said.

She turned her back, and watched him change in a mirror.

Charlie did as he was told. They fitted.

"You're in good shape, even though you obviously like a pint," said the woman.

"Am I?" said Charlie, surprised.

"Yes, very nice. A suit suits you. I might have to make a few alterations, but I can easily do that. I'm fully equipped."

Charlie quite liked the sound of that. And he liked her. She was rather pretty in a tired sort of way. Experienced.

Ah, now he placed her, and the grand piano.

"I know you from the regatta committee," he said.

"Yes, we met there. I'm social secretary."

"An estate agent... "

"Indeed. My name's Sally, and you're Charlie. You work for the Chronicle and you flew that flying machine thing. And you saved that farmer from a bull. It was in the paper. Very brave. A nice photo of you, I thought."

"Oh, thanks."

He was quite shocked. She thought he was brave! And looked nice in a photo!

He didn't know what to say. – "Oh, um, who did the suits belong to?"

"My husband. He's left me, you know. After 20 years. We were childhood sweethearts. He just walked out. With another man."

"He wasn't the Director of Piers, Parks and Pubic Places was he?" said Charlie.

She laughed – "You know him?"

"Only by reputation. He was bosom buddies with my editor."

"It leaves a vacancy," said Sally.

"On the council?"

"I'll show you the rest of the house," said his hostess, laughing. "There's quite a lot on offer."

And there was.

Also in Nettle Books:

Flying with a Broken Wing
Sat Mehta

Flying with a Broken Wing tells the true story of a boy growing up in India in turbulent times. Sat Mehta was five years old when he and his family became refugees, caught up in the biggest migration in modern history at the time of Independence. His home was destroyed, his uncle murdered. Once very wealthy farmers, the Mehtas became destitute. Later, Sat suffered a broken arm – complications set in and amputation seemed inevitable. As he lay in hospital, a world famous surgeon, Professor Robert Roaf, strode onto the ward, choosing "hopeless cases" to help. Sat got a second chance.

£10. ISBN 978-0-9561513-2-2

Branwell & Other Stories
Michael Yates

Branwell is the story of the Bronte boy who once ruled an imaginary childhood world. As an adult, he fails as a poet and painter, is doomed in love and literature, and slips down the road of drink, drugs and despair. Plus five other stories by this contemporary writer.

£9. ISBN 978-0-9561513-4-6